Sleek. Dead black. She could fly twenty miles high, travel two thousand miles without refueling, at three times the speed of sound. The Air Force's fastest fighting plane, the Mach 3 Arrow.

Despite himself, Sarko felt a thrill. He walked slowly alongside the plane and put out a hand to touch the smooth black metal that he had created. It had taken six years of his life to make that metal perfect.

Sarko and Colt climbed a metal staircase to a catwalk that ran around to the farthest end of the hangar. There they could look down into a section that had been screened off from the main hangar floor.

Sarko looked down, and felt sick. "What ... what happened?"

Spread across the floor was the wreckage of a Mach 3 Arrow.

Sarko felt his temper blaze up. "I told you, the metals are all right! It's not the metals!"

"You told me what you *believe*," Colt snapped. "But you don't know for sure. *Maybe you killed those men. And maybe your supersonic transport plane will kill hundreds of people, if you don't find out what's wrong with the Arrow. Ever thought of that?*"

OUT OF THE SUN

BEN BOVA

A TOM DOHERTY ASSOCIATES BOOK

A Tor Book

Published by Tom Doherty Associates, 8-10 W. 36th St., New York City, N.Y. 10018

First printing, February 1984

Cover art by: Jim Gurney

ISBN: 812-53-210-4
ISBN: Can. Ed. 812-53-211-2

Printed in the United States of America

OUT OF THE SUN

Out of the Sun is dedicated to the men and women in the laboratories who do the work that leads to planes that can fly faster, higher, farther, and more safely.

CHAPTER ONE

The fighter plane was nicknamed Arrow One. It was cruising eight miles high above the frozen white of the Arctic Ocean, not far from the North Pole.

Hundreds of miles away, the long-ranged radars on the coast of Alaska picked up an unknown bomber. Ground command sent Arrow One to check on it.

"Got him," the radar man said to the pilot, and he pointed to the screen in the middle of his control panel.

The pilot, sitting on the left side of the two-man cockpit, glanced at the blip of light on the radar screen. He pushed the throttles forward and winged over toward the oncoming bomber.

Arrow One raced ahead at Mach 3, three times the speed of sound. Within minutes the bomber was in sight.

"No markings on him," the pilot muttered. "Better radio back to ground command that . . ."

He never finished the sentence.

Arrow One fell apart. Instantly. No warning, no chance of escape. The plane shattered into a thousand pieces. The pilot and radar man were dead before they could take another breath.

Paul Sarko edged along the narrow aisle of the big jet airliner. His suitcase felt heavy and clumsy. He held it out in front of himself so that it wouldn't bang on the seats as he walked through.

He smiled at the stewardess who was standing at the main hatch, then ducked through into the bright springtime sunlight.

Standing at the bottom of the stairs, squinting up at the passengers as they left the plane, was Dr. Ratterman. Sarko hurried down the stairs and shook hands with his ex-boss.

"Hello, Leon! You finally finished building your swimming pool, didn't you?"

Dr. Ratterman looked surprised. Then his hand went up to touch his tanned and peeling bald head.

With a smile, he said, "You're still a detective, Paul."

Sarko laughed. He had a roundish face with large, alert, dark eyes that seemed to probe everywhere. His hair was straight and black. He was a lanky, restless six-footer; much bigger than the short, thin Dr. Ratterman.

A jet roared off from the runway as they started across the airport parking apron. Dr. Ratterman pointed toward an Air Force helicopter standing off to one side of the terminal building.

Sarko's eyebrows hitched upward. "You must be in a hurry, Leon."

The older man nodded, dead serious now. An Airman ran up to them and took Sarko's suitcase. They followed him to the 'copter and climbed in. The pilot started the engines as they strapped themselves into the bucket seats. As soon as the Airman had hopped aboard, they lifted straight up.

"Why all the mystery on the phone?" Sarko asked, over the whine of the turbine engines. "What's so important that you have to yank me away from my job? And why me, anyway? I'm not . . ."

Dr. Ratterman waved him into silence. "You'll see in a few minutes."

The 'copter cut straight across a small town and out over several miles of farmland. Then the huge runways of the air base slid into view. Beyond them was a fair-sized city of gray cinder-block buildings and white frame houses and barracks. Sarko knew every building, inch by inch. Especially the research labs. He had spent six years of his life there. He had left nearly a year ago, thinking that he'd never come back.

They landed at the far end of one of the runways, next to a giant hangar.

"They'll take your luggage," Dr. Ratterman said,

nodding at the Airman and pilot. "You'll be living on the base for the time being."

"For the time being?" Sarko began to feel uneasy as he climbed down from the helicopter to the cement paving. "What's this all about, Leon? What's the secret? I had a good job in Seattle, and now . . ."

But Dr. Ratterman didn't answer. He headed for the hangar. Sarko had no choice except to follow him.

Through a set of double doors. An Air Policeman stood between the doors, with an automatic pistol strapped to his hip. Inside . . .

The Arrow.

Sleek. Dead black. Two huge fan-jet engines with afterburners. Stubby, swept-back wings. Flat-bottomed delta-shaped body squatting on three sets of triple wheels. She could fly twenty miles high, travel two thousand miles without refueling, at three times the speed of sound. The Air Force's fastest fighting plane, the Mach 3 Arrow.

Despite himself, Sarko felt a thrill. He walked slowly alongside the plane and put out a hand to touch the smooth black metal that he had created. It had taken six years of his life to make that metal perfect.

"This is the first time you've seen her, isn't it?" Dr. Ratterman's voice rang hollow in the vast, quiet hangar.

Sarko nodded.

"She's your baby, as much as anybody's."

Sarko turned on the older man. "No, she's not! She's a weapon. I didn't work on a weapon. I did a research job. I just wanted to make a metal alloy that would stand up to Mach 3 speeds. You turned the metal into a weapon. The Arrow is yours, not mine."

"All right," Dr. Ratterman said, raising his hands. "All right. So now you're out of the Air Force and working on Mach 3 airliners."

"I was—until you drafted me. What did you tell my boss? He looked as though World War Six had just hit him."

Instead of answering, Dr. Ratterman said, "Come up here with me."

They climbed a metal staircase to a catwalk that ran around the inside walls of the hangar. Their footsteps clanked on the metal deck. Dr. Ratterman led Sarko back to the farthest end of the hangar. There they could look down into a section that had been screened off from the main hangar floor.

Sarko looked down, and felt his knees wobble. "What . . . what happened?"

Spread across the floor was wreckage. There wasn't enough left to tell what the plane had looked like before its crash, except that it probably had been painted black, and might have had stubby, swept-back wings.

"It's an Arrow." Dr. Ratterman said flatly. "We've built four. That was the first one. She crashed over the Arctic Ocean two weeks ago. That's all the Navy could find of her. The rest is at the bottom of the ocean."

Sarko leaned forward and grabbed the handrail in front of him with both fists. For a moment he thought he was going to be sick.

13

"It . . . how did it happen?"

Dr. Ratterman shook his head. "That's why we need a detective. A detective who knows about the metals in that plane. Two more Arrows are flying right now. You saw the fourth one when we came in here. We've got to find out why this one crashed . . . and make sure the same thing doesn't happen to the other three."

CHAPTER TWO

They walked in silence out of the hangar, into the hot sunlight. A million questions were boiling in Sarko's mind, but he didn't speak. It was too much. Six years of work lying twisted and smashed on the bare floor of the hangar. What had gone wrong?

They climbed into a waiting jeep and drove off along the two-mile-long runway toward the control tower. A huge B-52 scorched down the runway, its engines screaming and pouring out black smoke.

It lifted off the ground just as it passed alongside them. The thunder of its engines was so loud that Sarko could *feel* the noise as well as hear it. And down at the far end of the runway, another plane was already starting to roll through the haze of the bomber's exhaust fumes. It was a KC-135 tanker, filled with kerosene for a mid-air refueling of the B-52, thousands of miles away.

Sarko saw the planes take off, and heard them, and felt the blasts of wind they made. But his thoughts were still in that hangar. He was still looking at the wrecked Arrow, still hearing Dr. Ratterman's voice, ". . . and make sure the same thing doesn't happen to the other three."

The jeep stopped near the control tower. Dr. Ratterman stepped out first and pointed toward a two-story building.

Sarko followed him inside. The air conditioning made him shiver slightly as they hustled up the steps to the second floor. Dr. Ratterman walked halfway down the long, drab hallway and stopped at a door marked Maj. F. D. R. Colt.

He knocked once and was already turning the knob when the voice from inside said, "Come in."

"Hello, Doc," Major Colt said. "This is your friend?"

Dr. Ratterman nodded. With a wave of his hand, he introduced the two men to each other.

Major Colt was sitting behind a gray metal desk. The only other furniture in the room was a metal bookcase, a gray filing cabinet and two chairs. There were no windows in the tiny office; the walls were covered with maps.

The Major stood up and reached for Sarko's outstretched hand. He was about Sarko's age, a little taller, and much bigger in the shoulders and chest.

16

He wore the wings of a flier on his blue jacket. His skin was a smooth, dark coffee color. He had a high forehead, a broad face, and a quick, bright smile.

"Sit down," Major Colt said. "Is it Mr. Sarko or Doctor Sarko?"

"It's Doctor," Sarko answered as he sat down, "but I'd rather be called Paul."

"So you did the structural engineering for the Arrow," the Major said, cupping his chin in his hands.

Sarko replied, "I did the research work on the metals that went into her. I didn't do any design work."

"I showed Paul the wreckage," said Dr. Ratterman. Major Colt nodded.

"You think it's some sort of structural problem with the plane?" Sarko asked.

"Don't know." The Major shrugged. "We have four-teen dozen different kinds of experts working on the problem. Doc here wanted you to handle the struc-tural end of it."

"Not structural, exactly," Dr. Ratterman corrected. "Material. The metal alloys in that plane are mostly new, never been flown before. They tested out all right in the laboratory and wind tunnels, but . . ."

"But they might have fallen apart in flight," Sarko finished the thought.

"It's possible," Major Colt said.

Sarko shook his head. "Not really. There's nothing wrong with those metals. I know it and Dr. Ratterman knows it."

"But Paul . . .," Dr. Ratterman began.

Major Colt stopped him. "Wait a minute, Paul.

17

You could be right. But we just don't know. We don't know why she crashed. And we've got to find out. Fast."

"There must be two hundred materials and structural engineers in the labs here on the base. Why drag me in?"

"Because that's *your* metal in the Arrows," the Major answered firmly.

"Hold on now. Just because . . ."

"Listen," Colt said, getting up from his desk chair. "This isn't just an ordinary plane crash. The Arrow is supposed to be the best fighter plane in the world. And something's wrong with it. Maybe it fell apart in mid-air. Maybe it's a flying death-trap."

Sarko didn't answer.

"But what's even worse," said the Major as he walked around the desk, "is that the plane might not have simply crashed. She might have been shot down."

"What?"

Pointing to the Arctic on a map on the office wall, Major Colt explained.

"Look. We've been flying patrol over the Arctic for years, and so has the other side. They know we have supersonic bombers, so they've put up supersonic fighters to show us that our bombers couldn't get into their country without a fight. We've also seen their bombers around the North Pole. Their newest ones fly twice as fast as sound—Mach 2."

Sarko shrugged. "So?"

"So we built the Arrow and sent it out over the Arctic to show them that their bombers can't get past our newest fighter."

"It sounds like some kids' game," Sarko said, frowning.

"It's a game, all right," answered Colt. "A dead serious game. Now our newest fighter has crashed. Okay, it was only one plane. But there was a bomber from the other side on the scene when the Arrow went down! One of our long-range radars picked it up. What if they've got a bomber that can shoot down our fighters so easily that they can get through our defenses and bomb us? They might start a war this afternoon!"

"But we've got other defenses," Sarko said. "What about our antiaircraft guns and missiles . . ."

Colt shook his head. "If they can get past the Arrow, I'd bet that their bombers can get past anything else we've got. That's why we've got to know why Arrow One crashed. *We've got to know!*"

The phone on his desk buzzed. Major Colt picked it up. After a few words, his whole body seemed to stiffen. His face went blank with shock. Without another word, he slowly put down the phone.

"What is it?" Dr. Ratterman asked.

Colt blinked a few times before he could find his voice. "Arrows Two and Three. They're down—both of them—over the Arctic."

"Down?" Sarko snapped. "You mean crashed?"

Colt nodded, his eyes still wide and unbelieving. "According to the report, there was another plane in the area. DEW-line and BMEWS radar both spotted it. Not one of our planes. The two Arrows went over to see what it was, and . . . and they crashed."

CHAPTER THREE

Paul Sarko lay stretched out on the bed of his room, in the unmarried officers' quarters of the base. He was fully clothed and wide awake. His hands were clasped behind his head and he was staring at the ceiling.

It's not the metals, he told himself. It couldn't be; they were tested for years before the plane was built. Wind-tunnel test, stress tests, fatigue tests, heat tests . . .

There's nothing wrong with the metals! Sarko told himself again. Whatever happened to the planes, it happened because of enemy action. So there's nothing I can do, and they shouldn't expect me to hang around here for nothing.

He sat up on the bed. It was dark outside, and he realized that he was hungry.

Taking the telephone from the table, he got the number for Thornton Airlines from directory services then made a reservation on the next day's flight back to Seattle.

An hour later, he was sitting in a booth at the base's officers' club. He had finished his dinner and held a half-empty coffee cup in one hand. A six-piece band was blasting away at the far end of the room. People were dancing and listening. Sarko beat time to the music with his free hand.

"You look relaxed."

Sarko looked up and saw Major Colt.

"Is that against the law?" Sarko had to raise his voice to be heard over the pounding music.

The Major shook his head. "No . . . not for civilians, anyway. Mind if I sit down?"

Before Sarko could answer, the Major had slipped into the booth across the table from him.

"You might as well know," Sarko said, "I'm leaving on tomorrow's plane."

Colt's eyes locked on Sarko's. "Leaving?"

"I've spent the whole afternoon thinking about it. There's nothing wrong with . . ."

"Don't say it!" Colt hissed. "Remember, the whole business is Top Secret."

Sarko pointed to the bandstand. "Everybody's listening to them. Besides, you can barely hear yourself think."

21

"Just the same," Colt said, hunching over the table, "don't say anything you shouldn't."

"Well, I'm leaving anyway," Sarko repeated. "It's not my problem. There's nothing wrong with my end of the job."

"You know that for sure, huh?"

"I'm certain of it."

"One hundred percent certain," Colt said. "Not even curious enough to see if you're right or wrong? You think the lab work and the wind-tunnel tests are right and what's happened the past few days is a bad dream?"

"Now wait a minute . . ."

"If you ask me," Colt went on, "I'd say that there just might have been something missing from those wind-tunnel tests, something that didn't show up until those planes had been flying for a while."

"What do you mean?"

"Never mind." Colt got to his feet. "Like you said this afternoon, we've got two hundred materials engineers around here. We don't need one more. Not you, anyway."

He turned and walked away. Sarko watched him leave the club.

For more than an hour, Sarko sat in the booth alone, turning thoughts over and over in his mind. At last he got up. He called Base Information and found out that Colt lived on the base, in the married officers' quarters.

It was a long walk, but the night was warm and calm. The married officers' quarters made up a little village within the base: small, white clapboard houses set neatly on a grid of wide streets. The smell of freshly mown lawns hung in the air. A few scrawny trees stood along the sidewalks, and Sarko could see children's swings and bikes out in the backyards and driveways. The houses were all built exactly alike, but in the soft moonlight they looked almost pretty.

He found Colt's home. The lights were still on downstairs, so he knocked on the front door.

Mrs. Colt came to the door. She was slim and pleasant-looking, her dark skin a good contrast to the bright-colored dress she was wearing.

"Is the Major in? I'd like to see him. I'm Paul Sarko."

She looked surprised for a moment, then puzzled. But she said, "Come on in, I'll call him." There was a hint of the South in her voice.

She showed Sarko to the small but comfortable living room, then excused herself and went to the kitchen. In a moment, Colt came in. He was wearing a sport shirt and slacks.

"I wasn't expecting a visit from you," he said. He looked wary, on guard.

Sarko said, "I . . . I think I owe you an explanation."

"Sit down, sit down." Colt pointed to the sofa. He pulled up a rocker for himself as Sarko tried to relax on the sofa.

"Would y'all like something to drink?" Mrs. Colt asked from the doorway.

"How about some beer?" the Major suggested.

Sarko nodded. "Sounds fine."

Mrs. Colt soon returned with the frosty glasses. Then she went upstairs. The Major said, grinning:

"She knows we'll be talking about Air Force business, and she shouldn't hear it. Gets her awfully curious, though."

"Look," Sarko began, without any buildup. "I don't want you to think that I'm just running out on you. Or that I'm afraid that I'd find that my metals caused the crashes."

Colt took a sip of beer. "Okay, just why are you going?"

"I made a decision," Sarko said, still feeling nervous, "more than a year ago. I decided that I'm finished with Air Force work."

"Oh?"

"I spent six years with Ratterman, working on those alloys. I came straight out of the university to this base. For six years I worked on making metals that would allow a plane to fly steadily at Mach 3. Okay, you've got the metals now and you can do whatever you want with them. You can make fighters or bombers or missiles or anything you want. You can use them in that game you play over the Arctic."

Colt looked at him oddly, but said nothing.

"Six years of my life is enough," Sarko went on. "I want to do other things now. I want to help build transport planes that can fly at Mach 3. Or maybe work on something completely different. There's more to the world than making war planes!"

"Sure," Colt said softly. "But we've got a bad problem on our hands and we need you to help us find the answer."

A mosquito buzzed by Sarko's ear and he waved his hand to chase it. "But it's not my problem!"

"You're half right," Colt said. "It's an Air Force problem, and we can't force you to help us. But if they've got a bomber than can knock down the Arrow . . ."

"I know, I know . . . you'll want to figure out some way to stop their bomber. Another move in your game."

"We've got to balance the books, Paul," Colt said seriously. "It's a lesson I learned a long time ago. The other side has got to respect you, or else he'll push you around as much as he can. Right now, the other side thinks they're one move ahead of us. They've knocked down three of our best planes. We've got to show them that they're not ahead of us. If we don't show them, then we—all of us, including you—we're in deep trouble."

"I don't like your game," Sarko said.

The mosquito buzzed into view again and settled on the side of Colt's neck. With a lightning-like *crack!* he crushed it in his open palm.

"I don't like the game either," the Major said, scraping the bug off his hand and into an ash tray. "But it's something like this bug. Let him have his own way and he'll take the blood out of you. So you stop him."

"By killing him."

"Sometimes that's the only way to do it. But don't think that you have to fire a gun or fly a fighter plane to kill people."

"What do you mean?"

25

Colt edged forward tensely. "How do you know that *you* didn't kill those six men?"

Sarko felt his temper blaze up. "I told you that the metals are all right!"

"You told me what you *believe*," Colt snapped. "But you don't know for sure. Maybe you killed those men. And maybe your supersonic transport plane will kill hundreds of people, if you don't find out what's wrong with the Arrow. Ever thought of that?"

Sarko started to answer, shut his mouth, finally spat out, "That's the lowest blow of all!"

Colt shrugged. "We're at war, buddy. All's fair."

With trembling hands, Sarko put his glass down on the coffee table. "All right, Major. You win. I'll stay and help you find out why the planes crashed. And the minute I do, I'm leaving here so fast that your head will spin."

Colt stood up. "I'll keep a helicopter waiting for you, so you won't have to waste any time. . .*after* you've found the answers we need."

Sarko got to his feet and angrily stormed out of the house.

CHAPTER FOUR

The radio announcer was saying, "It's a perfect afternoon for baseball . . . bright and warm. The weatherman promises beautiful weather right through the Memorial Day weekend, as the Reds take on the Dodgers for a big four-game series . . ."

"Why don't you turn that thing off?" Paul Sarko asked.

At the other desk in the small office, Martin Arnold clicked the transistor radio shut. With a sad shake of his head, he put the little black portable into a drawer.

"It's too nice a Saturday to work," he said.

Sarko glanced out the room's one window. It was a fine day. The base was practically deserted.

"You can go if you want to," he said to Arnold.

Martin Arnold was about Sarko's age. He was a shade shorter than Sarko, and starting to get puffy around the middle. He had a long face, with a big toothy grin. His high forehead made him look as though he was starting to go bald.

He wasn't grinning at the moment. Looking out the window, he said, "We could get to the ball park in time to see the second game."

Sarko shook his head. "No thanks. Not me. There's too much to do here."

The room was air conditioned, but the two engineers were in their shirtsleeves. Sarko had his rolled up. His desk was covered with papers, reports, photographs, and his notes. A movie projector was set up on a table behind his desk, aimed at a screen that covered the opposite wall next to Arnold's desk.

Looking at Arnold again, he said, "Listen, Marty, you can go if you want to. Nobody's keeping you here. When I asked for you to be my assistant on this job, I didn't expect you to work seven days a week."

"But you do," Arnold said.

Sarko shrugged.

"And you've been working just about twenty-four hours a day. Paul, you've got to rest! You've been driving yourself for two weeks now ... you can't keep going on like this much longer."

"General Hastings is calling a meeting Monday to review the progress we've made on the problem," Sarko said wearily. "Ratterman, Colt, and all the experts. I want to have something concrete to tell them. Not just another round of bland stares."

Rubbing his high forehead, Arnold said, "But we've been over every scrap of information dozens of times. There's nothing new. We just don't have enough to go on!"

Sarko frowned. Then, in quiet voice, he asked, "Marty . . . you worked with me for more than two years on the Arrow's metals. What do you think? Did I goof somewhere? Did the metals cause the crashes?"

For a long moment Arnold didn't answer. "I can't really tell, Paul," he said at last, his eyes avoiding Sarko's. "My honest feeling is that the metals are okay; but I don't have any evidence to back up that feeling."

"I guess you're right . . ."

"There's no real evidence the other way either," Arnold quickly added. "Nothing to show that the metals failed."

"There's no real evidence of anything!" Sarko slammed his hand on the desk top. "Radar tracking showed the planes operated normally . . . until the instant they broke up.

"The wreckage we've got back shows everything was normal. Controls were okay, fuel okay, engines okay . . . nothing wrong anyplace. But the planes crashed."

"Whatever happened," Arnold said, "happened in an instant."

"I know," Sarko agreed. "Not like a normal emergency in a plane. Usually there's time for the pilot to try something, or at least to hit the eject button and

29

get out of the plane. But here . . . one minute everything's fine, and an instant later—the plane's fallen apart."

"Maybe they were hit with a small nuclear warhead?"

"No," Sarko shook his head. "There are no signs of blast, no radioactivity. Besides, the ground radars would've picked it up."

"Small high-explosive shells? They wouldn't have to hit the plane, just go off close enough to knock it out of control."

"Then why didn't the pilot get the plane back under control? Out of the three planes, at least one of them should've been able to do it. And why did all the planes fall apart? Why didn't the electronics men get off some kind of message? Even if a plane's power-diving, it takes a few seconds to get down to sea level. Somebody should've hollered *something!* Even the movie film that the Navy recovered from Arrow Three blanks out just when the trouble happens."

With a nod of his head, Sarko leaned across his desk and punched the ON button of the tape recorder there. The speaker crackled and hummed for a few moments. Then the voice of the Arrow Three crewman said:

"We've made visual contact with the bogey . . . delta-winged . . . looks like four engines on her. Definitely a long-range bomber. We're both moving in closer. Arrow Two is in the lead, we're foll . . . Omygod! She's hit . . . she's falling apart! Flash . . ."

The rest of the tape was a garbled mixture of sounds:

perhaps voices, perhaps screams. It ended in less than three seconds.

Arnold looked pale as Sarko turned off the machine.

"Every time I hear it, it bothers me," Arnold said, his voice trembling slightly.

"Most of the structures people on the base think that the metals failed," Sarko said grimly. "They figured out that all three planes crashed after just about the same number of hours of flying time. They're talking about sonic fatigue, or heat fatigue, or whatever kind of fancy name they can think up for it."

"But the guy on the tape said Arrow Two was hit with something," Arnold said.

Shrugging, Sarko answered, "They figure that when he saw the plane start to fall apart, he got excited and thought the enemy plane was shooting at them."

Arnold said nothing.

"What bothers me, though," Sarko went on, "is the last word on the tape that you can hear clearly. Sounds like 'Flash.' What did he mean by that? And why did the movie film blank out—just about at the same instant, too?"

"It doesn't make any sense," Arnold said.

"Not yet," Sarko agreed. "We don't have enough information."

"And we're not going to get any more. Arrow Four is grounded."

"I know. But maybe we can squeeze more information out of what we've already got."

"We've been through it for two weeks straight now. There's nothing new to find," Arnold said.

"Maybe," Sarko said. "Maybe. But there must be

something. What about the medical report? They found one crewman out of the six. What about him? What killed him?"

Arnold shook his head. "That's not our ball park. They probably wouldn't tell you about it if you asked."

Sarko reached for the phone, then stopped. "Probably nobody over at the medical building this afternoon who can give me the report."

"Come on, Paul," Arnold said. "All you're going to get out of this is a king-sized headache. Let's take the rest of the afternoon off and see that ball game."

"You go, Marty. I want to think about this some more."

CHAPTER FIVE

The meeting the next Monday was very much like the meetings of the two Mondays before: long, and—to Sarko—pointless.

The conference room was crowded, hot, and stuffy. General Hastings kept chewing his cigar and saying that something had to be done. The experts kept repeating that there was no new information, no new ideas.

One or two of the men at the long conference table said that the only possible answer was that the metals had somehow failed.

"How?" asked the General.

No one knew.

"Dr. Sarko, you're the expert on metals," the General called down the table. "What's your story?"

"I've reviewed all the tests we've ever made on those alloys," Sarko answered. "According to everything we know, the metals are okay."

"But suppose there's something that we don't know about?" the General asked sternly.

Sarko glanced at Dr. Ratterman, then looked back at the General. "General Hastings, there's obviously *something* here that we don't know about. And that something caused the crash. But it wasn't the metals. I'm sure of that."

The meeting dragged on for another hour, then finally broke up. The General's last words were:

"If you don't find the answer soon, we might all end up doing our work in bomb shelters, because the Reds will be able to fly their bombers anywhere they choose to!"

As Sarko left the building where the conference had been held, Major Colt called to him.

"Going to lunch?"

"Not yet," Sarko answered. "I want to get the medical report on the crewman they found."

Colt fell in step alongside him and they walked across the parking lot toward the hospital building.

"You onto something?" asked the Major.

With a shake of his head, Sarko replied, "Just grabbing for straws . . . anything."

Colt was silent for a moment. Then he asked, "You really sure that the metals didn't break up?"

"I don't have anything that shows that they failed."

34

"But you can't prove that they didn't fail."

"Now look . . ." Sarko began.

Colt held his hands up and grinned. "Hold it, hold it. I'm not trying to start a fight. I know there's not enough evidence to hang a cloud on . . . What I want to know is how you *feel*. Do you think the metals could have fallen apart?"

Sarko stopped walking and looked at the Major. He was serious, in spite of his grinning.

"I don't think it's the metals," Sarko said firmly. "Not by themselves, anyway. They didn't fail. Something might have been done to break them . . . but they didn't fail by themselves."

They started walking again. Colt said, "Most of the experts at the conference thought the metals failed."

"They don't know what else to say."

"I think you're right," Colt agreed. "But unless we do something to show them they're wrong, the blame's going to be put on the metals. And you'll get stuck with the job of proving it isn't true."

"How the hell can I . . ."

Grinning again, Colt said, "I've got it all figured out. They claim the metals fail after the plane's been flying a total of about a hundred hours at Mach 3. Okay. Arrow Four has logged about eighty hours at Mach 3. All I've got to do is put in twenty more hours, and we'll see if they're right or wrong."

"But Arrow Four's grounded," Sarko said.

"It is now. But I'm having lunch with the General. I think maybe I can get her flying again. I wanted to know how you felt before I sat down with the Old Man. See you later."

35

Major Colt turned and headed back for the General's office, leaving Sarko standing in the middle of the parking lot, staring at the blue-uniformed figure until it disappeared inside the building.

Only then did Sarko realize that the Major was offering to risk his life on the strength of a scientist's *feeling.*

Coming in from the hot, glaring parking lot to the cool, soft, green lobby of the medical building was a welcome change. After a few minutes of searching through the quiet hallways, Sarko found the office he was looking for.

It was a small outer office, with bigger rooms opening off doorways on either side. Seated at the office's only desk was a good-looking redhead.

"I'm here to pick up a report that Dr. Nash left for me," Sarko said to her.

The woman smiled prettily. The nameplate on her desk said R. Stefano.

"You're Dr. Sarko?" she asked.

"Paul Sarko."

"Well, I'm glad to see you!" she said. "I've been waiting nearly an hour. It was starting to look as if I'd miss lunch."

"On my account?" Sarko asked.

With a nod that tossed her red hair, she said, "This report you're picking up is Top Secret. I can't leave it just lying here. You've got to sign for it."

She pulled a thick envelope, big enough to hold a good-sized book, from the top drawer of her desk. Clipped to it was a white slip of paper, with several other papers of different colors underneath it.

Sarko looked it over, then signed his name.

"All right," the woman said, as she separated the different pieces of paper. "You keep the yellow one. I get the blue one. The white one goes back to the Security office."

Sarko lifted the heavy envelope. "Look," he said, "since I've made you wait so long, the least I can do is take you to lunch."

It took her only a moment to make up her mind.

"All right," she said, reaching for her handbag on the end of the desk. "I guess it *is* the least you can do."

Sarko laughed. "Right. Um, do I call you Miss Stefano or Mrs.?"

"Rita," she said. "Rita Stefano." She put the accent on the "a" in the middle of her last name.

Sarko opened the hallway door and they started for the cafeteria.

CHAPTER SIX

It took several days for Major Colt to get everything ready for Arrow Four's new series of test flights.

The first flight was set for that Thursday afternoon, but a chilly rainstorm swept the base with a blinding downpour. The next morning was still gray and damp, with big puddles along the runways and taxi ramps.

Paul Sarko found Major Colt in the pilot's locker room. Colt was surrounded by medical officers and technicians who were helping him into his high-altitude suit.

Sarko stood at the edge of the team of busy, muttering men. Colt, sitting on a stool, saw him and smiled.

38

"How's this for having a fuss made over you?" he asked.

Sarko nodded. "Not bad. But are you going to be able to take off with those clouds still covering the base? I thought you wanted to run the tests only in good weather."

As they stood him up to zip the sleeves and legs of the rubber-like pressure suit, Colt said. "Weather people claim the clouds'll lift off by noontime. It'll take us at least that long to get the plane and me both checked out. We'll fly in clear skies, I think. At least, that's the plan."

Sarko watched them put on the bright, metallic outer suit, then lace up the Major's boots. After they zipped on his gloves, Colt grabbed his plastic helmet and checked the oxygen line in its collar.

Finally the others stood back and the Major started toward the door.

"Let's go, Coach," he joked to Sarko. "I'm all set for the kickoff."

Laughing, Sarko said, "You look more like an astronaut than a football player."

"Except that the astronauts have air-conditioned buses to carry 'em to the rocket pad. All I've got is two size tens." Colt pointed to his boots.

They went down a hallway, through a door, and outside to the concrete ramp that connected the building with a row of hangars. The techs and medics followed behind them.

A little yellow tractor was towing Arrow Four out of its hangar. The plane reminded Sarko of a black panther, all coiled up and ready to spring.

"She looks eager to fly," Major Colt said as they walked up to the Arrow.

Sarko reached up and patted the plane's nose. "She was made to fly. She belongs in the air, not down here."

"You act as though you like this plane."

"I do."

"Even though she's designed to kill people?"

Sarko looked at the Major's face. He seemed curious, not mocking.

Turning back to admire the graceful sweep of the Arrow's lines, Sarko said, "She's built to fly higher and faster than anything with wings. The job you've put her to may be killing, but she's still the most beautiful plane in the world."

Colt shook his head. "Here I thought I was the only nut on the base who was in love with an airplane."

"You, too?"

The Major shrugged inside his glistening metal suit. "Sure. Why do you think I talked the General into letting me fly her? She's too good to sit in a hangar. She deserves to be up where she belongs."

"But if . . ."

"If there's anything wrong, we'll find out in another twenty hours of test time. It'll take about a week, if we stick to the schedule we've set up. About three hours a day of flying at Mach 3."

Sarko asked, "And then what?"

"I was talking to the Old Man about it this morning," Colt said, lowering his voice. "He thinks that if the test flights show that the metals are okay, then only two possible things could've happened to the other three Arrows."

"What are they?"

A B-52 roared overhead, hidden in the gray clouds. Colt waited, and thirty seconds later a KC-135 tanker added its thunder to the noise.

As the planes droned off into the distance, Colt said, "The General figures that either the other side has a weapon that we've never even thought of . . . or somebody's tinkering with the Arrows here on the ground."

"Tinkering?" Sarko's brows bunched into a puzzled frown.

"That's right. There could be a spy here on the base. Or more than one. In fact, I'd be surprised if there wasn't."

"You sound like somebody in the movies . . ."

Colt tapped the engineer's chest with a gloved finger. "Oh yeah? What about that cute redhead who's suddenly popped into your life?"

"Rita? But she's . . ."

"Do you really think that you're so great that a girl like that is going to be waiting for you whenever you feel lonesome?"

Sarko could feel his face getting hot. "Now wait a minute. I've only seen her a couple of times. There's nothing unusual about that!"

"She's had lunch with you three times this week, and Wednesday you took her to dinner and a movie."

"You've had me followed!"

Shaking his head, Colt answered, "It's a small town,

41

and the base isn't that big, either. We don't have to follow you to know what's going on."

Really angry now, Sarko had a hard time keeping his voice down. "You think that just because she's gone to lunch with me a couple of times she's a spy? That's . . . that's . . . it's the lousiest thing I've ever heard!"

"Cool it," Colt whispered. "I don't think anything. But anything's possible. *Anything* is possible. You could be a spy yourself."

"Or you could be," Sarko snapped.

The Major shrugged. "Okay, I could be. Does that make you happy?"

"You guys are really going off your rockers," Sarko fumed. "Spies! Next thing you know you'll be powdering the Arrow here for fingerprints."

"Just watch yourself, that's all," Colt said. "We're playing in the big leagues, and it's a rough game. I'm not the only one who could get hurt."

"That's for sure! A secretary can get run practically into jail just because she eats lunch with the same guy twice in one week."

"Three times," Colt said. Then he ducked under the Arrow's nose and walked back toward the cockpit. Sarko didn't follow him. He walked angrily away from the plane, back toward his office.

But when Arrow Four finally started rolling down the runway that afternoon, Sarko was standing at his office window, watching.

The skies had cleared, and the sunshine glinted off her black wings as she raced down the runway. Sarko felt his insides tighten as the plane lifted its nose off the ground. It ran a little way just on the two sets of main wheels and then seemed to hurl itself right off the runway.

Climbing at an impossible angle, Arrow Four rose cleanly and swiftly until Sarko could no longer see her, no matter how he stretched his neck at the window. He stood there, staring into the empty sky, waiting. Then it came. A sharp, sudden blast: the sonic boom. She was flying faster than sound now. Soon she would be at Mach 3.

There was not even the thin white line of a contrail to show where Arrow Four was; she was flying much too high for that.

Finally, with a last look at the blue sky, Sarko turned back to his desk. Back to the problem that had no answer.

Not yet.

But there were only three possible answers. Either the metals failed, or the planes were shot down by a new type of weapon, or there was a spy on the base.

CHAPTER SEVEN

Sarko worked right through the weekend. But it wasn't the kind of work he liked to do. It got him nowhere. It threw no new light on the problem.

He simply sat at his desk and read all the reports that had been written about the crashes. And reread them. And reread them, over and again.

He listened to the tape recording of the final few words from the Arrow Three crewman:

"She's hit ... she's falling apart! Flash ..." Then the screaming fall, until the tape suddenly went dead.

He watched the movie film salvaged from Arrow Three. It showed Arrow Two flying on ahead. Then the enemy plane came into view. Then the film went foggy and abruptly blanked out.

He walked over to the hangar where the wreckage of the planes had carefully been laid out, like the delicate bones of long-dead dinosaurs.

And he thought.

Read, listen, watch, walk, look, think. Read, listen, watch, walk, look, think.

And through it all, Sarko could hear the roar of Arrow Four's engines as Major Colt gunned her down the runway and into the air. Sonic booms rattled his office Saturday and Sunday afternoon.

On Monday, Sarko returned to the medical report of the crewman whose body had been found. Marty Arnold sat in gloomy silence at his desk as Sarko thumbed carefully through the thick report, with a medical dictionary at his elbow.

There was very little that was unusual in the medical report. The exact cause of death was uncertain, as it is in many aircraft accidents. But it appeared as though the man had been violently hurled out of an airplane that was falling apart.

He had suffered many broken bones, cuts, and bruises. His parachute had opened automatically, but he was probably dead when he left the airplane. He seemed to be flash-blinded, although he was not burned anywhere. The medical report concluded that he had probably looked directly into an exploding fuel tank.

Sarko raised his head and looked at Arnold.

"What is it?" the assistant asked.

45

"Did any of the reports you went through mention a fire on any of the planes?"

Arnold though a moment. "No, nothing about a fire."

"Could a fuel tank explode without showing any traces of fire in the wreckage?"

"I don't see how," Arnold said. "But remember, we don't have all of the wreckage. Most of it's at the bottom of the Arctic."

Sarko felt himself sag a little. "That's right. I forgot. So there could've been a fire after all."

Still, there was something here that wouldn't let go of him. Sarko stayed at his desk long after Arnold had quit for the day. He sat until the late spring afternoon had faded into twilight.

The ring of his phone snapped him out of his thoughts.

He picked up the receiver. "Hello."

"Paul?" It was Rita's voice. "I'm getting tired of waiting for you to show up before I can eat!"

Sarko suddenly remembered that he was supposed to take her to dinner. Quickly he glanced at his wristwatch. He was nearly an hour late already.

"I don't blame you for being upset! I'm sorry, Rita; I just lost track of time. Where are you now?"

"I'm at the Officers' Club."

"I'll be there in ten minutes."

He actually made it to the club in eight minutes. He spent most of the time during dinner soothing Rita's hurt feelings.

The band began playing and Rita wanted to dance.

After two fast numbers, though, Sarko was soaked to the skin.

"This isn't the thing for a man who's had a hard day," he gasped, while the band got ready for the next tune.

"A hard day? Sitting at a desk?" Rita laughed.

"Thinking can be tough work," Sarko said, leading her back through the crowd to their table.

Halfway there, he saw Major Colt and his wife coming toward them.

"Still following me?" Sarko asked. He smiled as he spoke, but he really didn't feel happy about it.

"I told you it's a pretty small world around here," answered Colt. "There's only one Officers' Club."

Sarko introduced Rita, who said, "Why don't you sit with us?"

"As long as the men promise not to talk business," Mrs. Colt said.

The Major laughed. "We'll behave. Honest."

As they sat at the table, listening to the music, Rita said to Sarko, "I hear you're a pretty good man with a banjo."

Grinning, Sarko admitted, "I used to be."

"How'd you hear about Paul's musical talents?" Major Colt asked.

Sarko stiffened in his chair.

Before he could answer, Rita replied with a smile, "As you said earlier, Frank, it's a small world here on the base. The word gets around. Some of the men I work for remembered Paul's sessions on the bandstand, before he left the Air Force."

47

Mrs. Colt said, "This is about the right time of night to get up there and join the band."

"Not tonight," Sarko said bluntly. "I'm afraid I'm not in the right mood."

There was a long moment of uncomfortable silence. At last, Rita said, "I've got to get home and take care of some laundry, or else I'll have to wear a blanket tomorrow."

They got up and walked slowly toward the door. The club had emptied now. The people who were still there were sitting up close to the bandstand, listening to an improvised jam session.

"How are the flights going?" Sarko asked the Major, his voice down nearly to a whisper.

"Fine," Colt whispered back. "She's behaving beautifully . . . sweet and pretty. Couple of more days and we'll be over the top."

"And then what?"

"Then we find out what *really* caused the crashes. And when we do . . ." Colt slowly squeezed his hand into a hard fist.

They went out to the parking lot together. The Colts drove off in their Datsun. Sarko let Rita drive him back toward his quarters in her car.

She said from behind the wheel as they drove through the darkness, "It seemed to me that you and the Major were . . . well, kind of edgy, like a couple of girls who showed up wearing the same dress."

Sarko didn't know what to answer.

Rita smiled. "Okay. I'll shut up."

They drove past the flight line, where rows of bombers, tankers, and transports were lined up. The big silvery planes looked ghostly in the darkness. A slight fog was creeping in, Sarko noticed, and it was cloudy overhead.

As Rita swung around a corner of the airfield, Sarko saw a pencil-thin beam of bright red light lancing up to the clouds.

"What's that?" he asked.

Rita glanced at it, then turned her eyes back to the road. "Some sort of new system for measuring the height of the clouds. They use it to help the control tower tell if the clouds are too low to allow planes to try landing, I think."

"It's a laser!"

"Yes," Rita agreed. "one of the control tower operators showed it to me when they first put it in. It's just a little thing, not much bigger than a flashlight. You wouldn't think it could throw such a bright beam."

"Stop the car." Sarko turned to Rita. "I've got to go to the city . . . can I borrow your car? I'll drop it off at your place."

"You're going right now?"

"Yes!" he said, excited. "I think I've got the answer I've been looking for! But I've got to check out a few points."

Rita pulled the car over and cut the engine. "What are you talking about?"

"Never mind. Just let me have the car. I'll leave it in front of your place when I'm finished with it."

"Oh no you won't," Rita said. "I'm going with you, wherever it is."

49

She opened the door on her side of the car. "Slide over, Paul. You can do the driving."

Sarko pushed himself across the seat. As Rita walked in front of the headlights, he slid the seat back to a comfortable distance from the wheel and snapped on the seat belt. As soon as Rita was belted into the right-hand seat, Sarko gunned the motor and raced off toward the city, some fifteen miles away.

"Where are we going, anyway?" Rita asked.

Sarko said, "To the nearest newspaper office."

CHAPTER EIGHT

"A laser?" Martin Arnold looked shocked. "That's crazy."

Sarko leaned back in his chair and watched his assistant.

"What's crazy about it?" he asked.

Arnold had just come in to work. He took off his jacket and hung it on the hook behind the office door.

"You can't shoot down a plane with a laser."

"Oh no?" Sarko asked. "Take a look at this."

He took a photocopy of a newspaper item from his desk and held it out to Arnold.

"I got it last night," he said, before his assistant could ask.

Arnold crossed the room and took the clipping. As he bent his head to read it, Sarko said excitedly:

"I thought I'd seen something about a laser shooting down a drone—a remotely piloted plane—out at the White Sands Test Range in New Mexico."

Arnold looked up from the clipping. His hand was shaking a little, Sarko saw.

"I heard about that test, too, Paul. They had to shine the laser on the drone for almost a full minute before it burned a hole through the plane's fuselage. And the laser they needed to do it weighed ten tons or more."

"That Russian bomber could carry a ten-ton laser."

Arnold's face went sour. "Maybe. But the Arrows were destroyed *instantly*, remember. They didn't sit there and let a laser take a minute or so to burn a hole through their skins."

Sarko admitted that with a rise of his eyebrows.

"And what would a little burn hole do to an Arrow?" Arnold demanded. "Nothing much. It sure wouldn't make the plane fall apart!"

"Yeah," Sarko muttered. "I guess not . . ."

"Besides, the alloys used on the Arrow were specifically designed to stand up to heat—lots of heat. I don't think a laser would do any damage to your alloys, Paul, unless it had *mucho*-megawatts of power and it could beam all that power onto one little spot of the airplane for minutes at a time."

Sarko nodded agreement.

"Which isn't the way it happened," Arnold insisted. "Not in any of the three crashes."

"But it's the best clue we have," Sarko countered. "In fact, it's the *only* real clue I've seen so far. And it ties in with the other points!"

Arnold went back to his desk and sat down. "What do you mean?" he asked softly.

"That medical report about the crewman being flash-blinded. And the tape recording . . . the last clear word on the tape is 'Flash.' Remember?"

"Yes, but . . ."

"And the movie film that blanked out. A laser beam could've caused that, too. It all fits."

Arnold shook his head. "It's crazy . . . wild . . ."

"Maybe so. But we're going to follow up on this idea. Fast."

"How?"

"There's no laser on the base powerful enough to use as a test device . . . But over at the state university they have one. We're taking a batch of samples of the Arrow's metals over there. This morning."

With a shrug, Arnold said. "Okay, you're the boss. But if I were you, I wouldn't go around telling everybody about this idea. It's pretty wild . . . and if it doesn't turn out to be right . . ."

"I know," Sarko agreed. "We'll keep it strictly between the two of us for the time being. We'll just tell the university people that we're doing some routine tests."

They drove out in Arnold's car later that morning.

The laser was a thick glass tube, and so long that it ran the entire length of the big laboratory room. It was surrounded by electric power generators and other equipment.

If this is what they're using against the Arrows, I can see why it takes a bomber to carry it, Sarko thought to himself.

"This is one of the most powerful capillary lasers in the country," the Professor told them as he guided them through his lab. "Of course, the gas-dynamic lasers are more powerful as a class of device, but even there, few of them put out as much power as we do."

He patted the glass tube like a proud father patting the tousled head of his son. A half-dozen technicians in white lab coats stood at one end of the room, waiting to turn on their equipment.

The professor was older than Sarko; his hair was beginning to turn gray. He was small and thin; he looked almost frail, but the little cuts and scrapes on his slim hands showed that he did a lot of the lab work himself.

The Professor looked at the plates Sarko held in his hands, then at Sarko and Arnold. "I hope you don't expect the laser to melt those. It isn't powerful enough. You'd need the kind the Air Force uses out at White Sands for that, and even then it would take several minutes."

Sarko said, "Do you remember the experiment done at M.I.T. a year or so ago, where they shattered solid rock with a laser beam?"

"Oh, yes!" The Professor's face lit up. "And their laser was only half as powerful as this one."

"I want to see what effect your laser will have on these metals," Sarko said.

"Probably none . . . or very little. Metals won't shatter the way rock does."

"I'd like to see what happens."

The Professor made them put on dark goggles and stand across the room from the laser tube. Two technicians placed one of Sarko's metal plates in a holder a few feet from the end of the laser tube.

When everything was ready, the Professor and his technicians went to a desk full of control dials and buttons.

"How long a run would you like us to try?" the Professor called over to Sarko.

"Five seconds."

"Very well."

The room suddenly filled with the hum of electrical power. Then, as the Professor touched buttons on the control panel, the long tube began to glow with a dull pinkish color.

"It's up to full power." one of the technicians said, without taking his eyes from the dials he was reading.

"Put the beam on the target," the Professor ordered.

Sarko looked at the metal plate as the technician called out, "One . . . two . . . three . . ."

Nothing much seemed to happen. The beam from the laser was infrared—invisible to human eyes. The metal itself seemed to be untouched, except for a slight warm-looking glow in the center of the plate.

". . . four . . . five."

The electrical hum stopped. The glow in the laser tube disappeared. The metal looked unchanged.

Sarko whipped off his goggles and rushed over to the metal plate. The Professor was right beside him.

"It looks exactly the same," the Professor said. "Untouched. Undamaged."

Sarko ran a hand over the metal. "It's warm, though. Some of the energy from the beam got into it."

"Really?" The Professor touched the plate. "You're right."

He turned back to one of the lab tables and found a magnifying glass. "Let's take a closer look."

The Professor peered carefully at the metal plate, then handed the glass to Sarko, saying, "It looks unchanged."

Sarko took the magnifying glass from him and had to agree that the metal seemed undamaged. The Professor led them to a laboratory down the hall, where they examined the metal under a powerful microscope. No damage had been done by the laser. The metal was as strong as it had been before the laser test.

As he and Martin Arnold left the university campus, Sarko felt almost happy. His metal alloy had stood up to a powerful laser without suffering the slightest damage.

But then he realized that he was no closer to a solution to the mystery of the Arrow crashes than he had been a month earlier.

CHAPTER NINE

"I was so certain that they used a laser," Sarko said, as Martin Arnold drove them back to the base.

Arnold glanced at Sarko. "It still sounds crazy to me. The thought of a supersonic bomber carrying a giant laser around, just in the hope that it'll meet one of our planes . . ."

"They knew we were flying Arrows over the Pole. They came looking for us."

"But the laser didn't do any damage. We still don't know why the planes fell apart."

Sarko sat quietly for a long while, watching the flat midwestern farmland go past the car's window, his mind churning over and over again like the wheels of the automobile. It *had* to be a laser, he thought. What else could it be? But how could a laser damage his metal? The alloy was created to absorb heat without losing its structural strength. Otherwise the Arrow could never fly at Mach 3 without . . .

"Airflow!" Sarko blurted.

"What?"

"We tested the metal against that laser in an ordinary room, at ambient temperature and pressure."

Arnold glanced at him. "Yeah. So what?"

"So the Arrow fell apart at high altitude," Sarko answered excitedly. "While flying at Mach 3!"

"What difference . . ."

"All the difference in the world," Sarko said, almost shouting. "Under Mach 3 conditions everything's different."

"Come on, Paul, it's not really . . ."

"We've got to do a laser test in a wind tunnel," Sarko insisted. "Not in the Professor's lab, but in the Mach 3 wind tunnel on the base."

"You're going to have a tough time convincing General Hastings of that."

"I know. It's not the kind of idea that he'll be able to swallow easily."

Frowning, Arnold said, "It'll take a couple of weeks, at least, to set things up."

"Not if I know Frank Colt," Sarko answered with a chuckle. "He'll get a team of men over there tonight and have the job done in a day or two."

Arnold slowed the car down. They were coming to the guard post at the base's main gate. The guard looked at the sticker on the car's windshield, then waved them on.

Putting on speed again, Arnold asked, "What do you want to do in the wind tunnel?"

"Show the General what happened," Sarko answered. "I think if we put one of our old test models of the Arrow in the wind tunnel and shine the laser on it, he'll see exactly what happened."

"You mean those little models we used a couple of years ago?"

"Right."

"Well," Arnold said, pulling the car into the parking slot next to their office, "I really think that all you'll be showing the General is what *might* have happened to the Arrows. If this laser scheme works, it still doesn't mean that that's what really happened."

Sarko stared at his assistant. "You mean it might have been something else?"

"Sure. I still think this laser idea is farfetched. Whether it works or not. And if you're barking up the wrong tree . . . we could end up with another crash."

Sarko thought it over for a long moment.

"You could be right," he said at last. "I got so excited about the laser idea that it never occurred to me that something else could be happening, too . . ."

"If I were you, I'd think things over pretty carefully before going to the General," Arnold said.

"Maybe I ought to sleep on it," Sarko agreed.

They went into the office.

"I'll write up the report on our visit to the university," Arnold said as he sat at his desk.

Sarko nodded and walked over to the window.

59

Arrow Four was barrelling down the runway, jets screaming.

"There he goes again," Sarko said at the black plane fired off into the sky. "He'll have his hundred hours by tomorrow, if all goes well."

Soon it was noontime and Arnold left for lunch. Sarko stayed at his desk, leafing through the piles of reports about the crashes.

He phoned the photo lab, where the film from Arrow Three was kept in a locked safe. About ten minutes later, one of the clerks brought the tiny spool of film in its red, TOP-SECRET-stamped can.

Sarko signed a Security slip for the film, and the clerk left. Then Sarko closed the window blinds. He threaded the film into the movie projector behind his desk and turned the machine on.

The screen across the room showed him what the camera on Arrow Three had seen: the dazzling white of the still-frozen Arctic Ocean, and a bit of the plane's own nose.

The plane was up so high that the sky was deep blue, and he could see the slight curve of the horizon. Arrow Two was in the picture, flying ahead of and slightly higher that Arrow Three.

Then, a few thousand feet below them, the other plane appeared. Triangle-shaped wings. Four pods for engines. A bomber all right. No doubt about it. Arrow Two dipped down toward it, and the camera —on Arrow Three—followed.

The other plane grew bigger and bigger. It was coming toward them, off to one side a little. Arrow Two lined up head-on with it, though, and . . .

The film suddenly snapped. The projector ran wildly, the loose end of the film slap-slap-slapping around in its reel.

Grumbling, Sarko turned off the projector and flicked the lights on. He took one look at the broken film and called the photo lab again.

The same clerk came back, with a film-splicing kit under his arm. He looked a trifle angry.

"Sorry if I cut into your lunch hour," Sarko said.

"We're shorthanded today," the clerk muttered as he took the film from the projector. "Bad enough I have to eat in the darkroom, but now I got to make house calls . . . Hey, this film's been cut."

"What?" Sarko stepped in close to see.

"Somebody's been cutting frames out of this film. See? Where it broke? It was cut and a couple of frames taken out. Then it was spliced back together again . . . by an amateur. Lousy splicing job. No wonder it broke."

"Forget the splicing," Sarko snapped. "Get back to the photo lab and get the list of everybody who's had this film. Everybody, do you hear!"

The clerk looked puzzled. "But why . . ."

"Never mind why. Just get moving! And call me as soon as you've got the list in your hand. Move!"

The clerk hurried out. Sarko paced nervously across the office until his phone rang.

"Dr. Sarko? This is the photo lab." The voice was the clerk's. "I've got the list of names . . . everybody who's run the film since it first came onto the base."

"All right, good. This is Tuesday. Now, who's had it since Sunday afternoon? I saw the film Sunday

61

and it was perfectly all right then, no frames missing, I'm sure. Who's had it since then?"

"Just you. You're the only man who's taken the film out of the photo lab."

"No one else has even seen it?"

"Nope. Just Mr. Arnold. He ran it through a couple of times this morning, early, but he didn't take it out of the lab. Said he was in a hurry ... said you and him was going to the university or something."

Marty Arnold. Sarko felt his insides grow cold.

"Was he alone when he saw the film this morning?" he heard himself ask.

The clerk thought a minute. "Yeah, we set him up in one of the workrooms."

One of the workrooms. Where he could snip a few frames out of the film and splice it back together again.

"Okay," Sarko said. "Thanks. I'll bring the film back in a few minutes."

He hung up. Without thinking about it, he put the spool of film back into its can. He mind was racing, picturing Arnold cutting the film.

"Where are the missing frames?" Sarko whispered to himself.

With his mind's eye, he pictured Marty Arnold quickly trying to splice the cut film together. Then he held the cut-out frames in his hand. What to do with them?

Sarko smiled grimly. He saw what Arnold had done.

Without wasting another second, he bolted for the door and headed straight for the photo lab.

CHAPTER TEN

"In the trash can?" The clerk was slightly amazed.

Sarko was on his knees, half buried in scraps of film and paper from the photo lab's workroom trash can.

"This is it," he shouted. "It's got to be!" He held up a curled, blackened sliver of film stock.

"It's been burned," the clerk said. "Who would, . . ."

Sarko squinted at the film, holding it up to the workroom's ceiling lights. The clerk peered at it over his shoulder.

"Can't see a thing," the clerk muttered. "It's ruined."

Grimly, Sarko answered, "Maybe not. Maybe not."

He headed for the door.

"Hey, wait! I got to get a receipt or something for those frames!"

"Later!" Sarko shouted over his shoulder.

He dashed all the way to the base's laser laboratory, where he spent nearly an hour talking the men there into doing what he wanted. Finally, after more talking and a good deal of work, they got things set up the way Sarko wanted them.

The burnt sliver of film was placed in a small holder in front of a laser. This laser not was like the one at the university; it was a tiny metal cylinder, no bigger than a flashlight. The room was darkened and the laser turned on. A pencil-thin beam of brilliant red light lanced through the blackened, curled piece of film.

Behind the film, in thin air, a tiny picture appeared. A three-dimensional, full-color picture, slightly larger than the image on the film itself.

Sarko leaned over into a half-crouch to see the little picture clearly. A technician squatted beside him.

"Very poor quality," the technician said. "Our holograms are a lot better."

"This one was taken by accident," Sarko murmured, more to himself than to anyone in the room. "Just a lucky freak accident . . . the lenses and camera were set up in such a way that when the bomber fired its laser at the plane, it put a hologram picture on this film."

Sarko had seen only a few hologram pictures before. They were the special type of pictures that lasers can make—usually without the need of a lens or camera at all. They were looking at the frames that the photo lab clerk had thought were burned and useless. They *were* burned, but despite that they still contained the special light pattern that formed a laser-made hologram picture.

"Lucky," he muttered. "But it's about time we got some luck running our way."

In the tiny picure—like a solid view hanging in mid-air, small but more real than any flat picture—Sarko saw Arrow Two, high above the gleaming white of the Arctic. He knew that the only reason he could see this picture was that Arrow Two had been exposed to a laser beam, and part of the laser's light had reached the camera on Arrow Three. So these pictures proved that a laser had been used to destroy the Arrows!

Arrow Two was starting to fall apart. Pieces were scattering everywhere. Sarko thought he saw shapes that looked like the plane's pilot and crewmen. One edge of the picture was glaring brightly, as though a light was starting to shine straight into the camera.

"Next frame."

"There's hardly anything left of the next frame," the technician said, as he carefully moved the fragile, brittle piece of film in its holder.

"That's okay," Sarko said. "Every part of a hologram, no matter how small, contains all the information in the hologram. That little slice of a frame will still show us the whole picture."

"Yeah," the technician said, "but the picture quality is just about gone."

Now the glare filled the picture. Nothing could be seen.

"That's it," the technician called out. "There's nothing else left."

Sarko knew that the rest of the film—sitting back in the photo lab now—was hopelessly burned out by the laser's brilliant light.

"Okay. Thanks."

The technician put on the lights and turned off the laser.

"Do you mind telling us what this is all about?" he asked. "What are we looking at?"

Sarko pulled the film from its holder in front of the laser. "Sorry, it's a big, dark—I mean, a big, *bright* secret."

After bringing the film safely back to the photo lab, though, Sarko didn't feel very cheerful. He started back toward his office. It was late afternoon now, nearly quitting time.

Martin Arnold had cut out those few frames from the film and burned them. He had done it after Sarko had told him his idea about the laser.

That meant Arnold *knew* there was an accidentally made hologram picture on the film. He had gone to the photo lab to destroy the one piece of evidence that proved beyond doubt that a laser had been used on the three Arrows.

CHAPTER ELEVEN

Arnold was sitting at his desk when Sarko burst into the office.

"Why, Marty? Why'd you do it?"

Arnold didn't seem too surprised. "Do what?"

"Cut the film from Arrow Three."

"You found it?"

"You must have known I would."

Sarko stood over his assistant, who looked up at him and said, "Paul ... I ... this is a hard place to talk. Somebody might come in, or the office might even be bugged with microphones. Can we go someplace else, where we can talk this whole thing through?"

"All right," Sarko said. "We can take a drive in your car. That ought to be private enough."

They went out to Arnold's car and drove off the base, heading for the wooded countryside beyond the housing development that clustered around the base.

"You tried to get rid of the only real evidence we have," Sarko said, "and even tried to make me think the laser idea was wrong."

"That's right, Paul. And I felt pretty bad about it. Question is, what are you going to do now?"

Sarko looked at him. "I ought to turn you over to Frank Colt. Or the Air Police."

"Without even knowing why I did what I did?"

"That's why I'm here," Sarko said. "To get your side of the story."

"There's not much to tell, really," Arnold replied, with a faint smile. "It all boils down to one thing— money."

"Money?"

"I owe money to everybody, Paul. This car isn't even paid for yet. I'm not a brilliant guy, like you are. I'm just an ordinary engineer. I needed money, more than I make at the base . . ."

"And you've been selling information?"

Arnold glanced at Sarko, then snapped his eyes back to the narrow, twisting road. "It started a few years ago, while you were still at the base full-time. A few people came to me . . . they said they were working for an aircraft company. They wanted to buy information about the metals we were working on."

"But didn't you think . . ."

"I didn't care. I figured, whoever they are, they just wanted information so they could make Mach 3 planes, too. They'd get the information one way or another, so why shouldn't I get paid for giving it to them?"

Sarko didn't know whether to be angry or sorry for him.

"I never knew that they were going to use the information to shot down the Arrows, Paul," Arnold said, still looking straight ahead. "Honest I didn't. They told me about it after the crashes, and told me to make sure you and Colt didn't catch onto the laser business."

"Marty . . . you've helped them kill six men!"

Arnold's face turned slightly red. "If it wasn't me, it would've been somebody else."

"And you want me to keep quiet about it?"

"Just for a little while, Paul. Long enough to let me get out of here."

Sarko slumped back in his seat, thinking hard.

"Just for a week or so," Arnold said. "Let me get out quietly, and then you can tell them about the laser. I'll be out of the country by then."

With a sudden shake of his head, Sarko said, "No, I can't do it. Frank won't wait another week. He knows there's nothing wrong with the Arrow. In another few days he'll fly Arrow Four out of here and go looking for trouble over the Arctic."

"Well . . . maybe you can stall him."

"Not Colt. He'll take that bird out over the Arctic and they'll kill him."

"Paul, give me a break!"

69

Sarko answered, "I can't, Marty. Not even if I wanted to."

Arnold slowed the car down and pulled it off to the side of the road. Sarko saw that they were at a crossroads. Another car was parked there, and Arnold stopped his car right behind it.

Before Sarko could say anything, a man appeared at the window beside him. He was tall, with a thin, bony face and curly blond hair.

"Well?" the man said to Arnold.

"No use," Arnold replied. "I tried to talk him out of it, but he won't listen."

"What is this, Marty?" Sarko demanded.

Arnold said, "I'm sorry, Paul. I tried to keep you out of this, but . . ."

CHAPTER TWELVE

The blond man said, "Outside, please."

Sarko glanced at Arnold, who shrugged unhappily and opened the door on his side of the car. Sarko grabbed the door handle beside him and pushed the door open.

In silence they walked to the other car: the blond man in front, Sarko next, Armold at the rear. *Like guards walking a prisoner*, Sarko thought.

The blond sat wearily on the front seat of his car and reached into the open glove compartment.

"I'm afraid, Dr. Sarko; that you're going to have a

fatal heart attack." He took a hypo needle out of a black case.

Sarko edged backward. "Now wait a minute . . ."

He bumped into Arnold.

"Hold him," the blond said.

Sarko felt Arnold's hands squeeze his arms. He looked around. The roads were deserted. There wasn't even a farmhouse in sight. A few birds were chirping in a clump of trees nearby and a plane or helicopter was droning lazily off in the distance.

"I'm sorry, Paul," Arnold was saying, almost babbling. "I didn't want it like this. Honest, I didn't think it would come to this . . ."

Sarko spun around, flashed out a fist at Arnold's face, and started running.

"Stop or I'll shoot!" he heard the blond shout.

He ran all the harder . . . for the trees. A pistol shot! He dove for the nearest clump of bushes. Nothing much, nothing that would stop a bullet. He could see them running toward him. The blond had a heavy black automatic in his hand.

Doubled over, trying to keep the bushed between himself and the gun, Sarko dashed toward the trees.

The gun cracked twice again, and Sarko saw wood splinter off the trees in front of him.

"You'll never make it, Sarko," the blond called out. "Stop now. The next shot will cut you in half."

Sarko stopped running and straightened up. The two men rushed toward him.

Suddenly the helicopter sound grew enormously louder. They all looked up and saw an Air Force 'copter skimming over the trees.

Arnold broke and ran back for the cars. The blond lifted his arm to fire, but the rattle of a machine gun churned the ground around him with blasts of dust. The blond was slammed down as though an invisible hand had flattened him forever.

The helicopter slid sideways over to the cars and landed in front of them. Arnold had his hands in the air as two Air Policemen jumped out with drawn guns.

Sarko felt his knees wobbling. He didn't move. He couldn't.

Another man in Air Force blue hopped out of the helicopter and starting running for him. Sarko recognized the dark face and bright grin.

"Just like the movies," Major Colt said, puffing a little.

"I'm not cut out to be a movie star, then," Sarko said.

"You okay?"

"No, I'm not. I don't think I'll ever be all right again," Sarko answered truthfully. "But I'm not hurt, if that's what you mean."

Colt put an arm around the scientist and they started back toward the cars and 'copter.

"They started playing rough," the Major said.

"Yeah." Sarko suddenly realized something. "Hey, how'd you get here? How'd you know . . ."

Colt laughed. "I told you we were worrying about a spy on the base. Then all of a sudden, this afternoon, you start hopping around like a flea at the dog pound. Photo lab, laser lab, back to the photo lab, and then out in Arnold's car."

73

"You *were* following me!"

"We were keeping an eye on everybody. But when you dashed off in Arnold's car, instead of going back to your quarters like a good citizen, I started worrying."

"You figured that I'd be in trouble." Sarko was slightly amazed at Colt's foresight.

The Major scratched his chin with his free hand. "Well . . . not exactly. I, um . . . I'm afraid that what worried me was the possibility that you were the spy we were looking for."

"Me?"

"Well, you were acting mighty strange."

"And you thought *I* was a spy?" Sarko pulled away from the Major and stood, still wobbly, on his own feet.

Colt's grin had turned a little sheepish. "I hated to think that you were the one. I was just starting to like you, really. But . . . well, put yourself in my place. If somebody started acting as nutty as you did this afternoon, what would you think?"

Sarko tried to frown, but found himself grinning back at Major Colt instead.

"Damned good thing you did follow me," he admitted.

Colt said, "I was starting to feel pretty rotten about this whole business when it looked like you were the guy we were after."

"Thanks."

They climbed into the helicopter together and sat behind the pilot. Arnold was in the rear seat, hand-cuffed and head down, with a grim-faced Air Police-man beside him. The other Air Policeman was checking out the cars and waiting for an ambulance to pick up the body of the blond man.

"At least I won't get any more warnings about going out with Rita," Sarko said as the 'copter's engines roared to full power for the liftoff.

"Boy, you took a wrong turn on that one," Colt's grin was wider than ever. "I wasn't warning you that she was a spy. I was trying to tip you off—without breaking Security rules—that Rita was the one who was watching you . . . for us. She's on our side!"

Sarko stared at the Major. "I guess that's real funny," he said lamely.

But he didn't laugh. He realized for the first time how much he enjoyed being with Rita. Now that Arnold was caught, there was no reason for her to see him again.

CHAPTER THIRTEEN

General Hastings peered into the thick glass port set into the side of the Mach 3 wind tunnel's test section.

Inside was a two-foot-long model of the Arrow. Further upstream, inside the wind tunnel also, was a big laser that had been flown in from White Sands.

The General chewed an unlit cigar. Turning to Sarko and Colt, who were standing with him on the metal catwalk that ran alongside the giant wind tunnel, he demanded:

"You really believe that a beam of light made those planes break up?"

"A very special kind of light beam," Sarko answered. "Together with the pressure of Mach 3 airstream."

The General shook his head and turned to Dr. Ratterman. "Leon, do you really think it's possible?"

"Our calculations show that it is," Dr. Ratterman answered softly. "This wind tunnel test should prove it, one way or the other."

With an unhappy frown, General Hastings grumbled, "All right, let's get on with it."

They clambered down the metal stairs to the main floor of the wind-tunnel building, then walked across to the control room. The wind tunnel loomed behind them like an immense steel pipe, studded with braces and bolts.

Glancing back at it, Sarko thought it looked like the body of a giant robot lying on its back. The spider web of stairs and platforms that ran alongside it showed how small human beings really were.

The control room was humming with quiet efficiency. Computer tapes spun, lights blinked, men moved smoothly about their jobs.

A TV screen showed the model of the Arrow. Sarko, Major Colt, Dr. Ratterman and the General stood in front of the screen.

"We're ready, Sir," the chief of the wind-tunnel crew said.

The General nodded.

From deep inside the building, the giant robot roared with the power of a thousand thunderstorms. The model in the TV screen looked unchanged, but now air was rushing over it at three times the speed of sound. The model was facing the same pressures and heat that the real Arrows did when they flew at their top speed.

"Laser ready, Sir."

General Hastings nodded again.

Sarko held his breath and counted to himself.

One, two, three, four. . . .

The model burst apart, as though a bomb had gone off inside it.

For a moment, no one moved. Even though Sarko had known what to expect, it was stunning. Finally the technicians began shutting down the tunnel. The roar died away. The lights on the control panels winked off.

General Hastings turned to Sarko. "So that's how they did it."

"Yes, Sir. By itself, the laser couldn't damage the alloy that the Arrow is built of. But with the pressure of a Mach 3 windstream blowing across that metal, a single sharp pulse of laser energy—a hundred million watts in a thousandth of a second—heats a tiny spot on the plane's skin tremendously. The alloy loses its structural strength at that one spot, and within seconds the weakness spreads out all through the skin of the plane. It just cracks apart like an eggshell."

"I want to thank you, Dr. Sarko. You've uncovered a very vital piece of knowledge."

"Question now," Major Colt said, "is how to defend Arrow Four against the laser."

"It shouldn't be too tough," Sarko said. "Actually,

it's not much of a weapon. It's bulky, and they probably can't fire more than two or three shots per mission."

"The success of the weapon depends on surprise," Dr. Ratterman said.

"That's right," Sarko agreed. "We can put a bright coat of paint on the planes, instead of the black they wear now. Then almost all of the laser beam will be reflected, even if it does hit the plane."

"And that will nullify their laser?"

"It will nullify the laser they're using now," Sarko said. "But lasers are getting more powerful, and more compact. They *are* the weapons of the future."

"Buck Rogers," the General snorted.

Sarko glanced at Colt, then went on, "General, it's only a matter of time before laser weapons make manned aircraft obsolete. They'll shoot down anything in the sky with the speed of light. What we've seen here today is just the beginning—the equivalent of the first fliers of World War I shooting at each other with revolvers."

General Hastings' craggy face seemed to go gray. "Thank God I'll be retired by then," he said.

Turning to Colt, he commanded, "Get Arrow Four ready as quickly as possible. I want it flying patrol over the Arctic right away. I want to show those people with the laser that we're wise to their game."

Colt smiled grimly. "Yes, *Sir*."

Sarko went back to his office. His real work was done. He had to write a report about it all, of course, but that was nothing.

He leaned back in his desk chair and gazed out the window at the perfect blue sky.

In his mind, he pictured Colt flying high over the Arctic, looking for the enemy plane. Colt was going to shoot it down. That would be his way to balance the score.

Then Sarko thought about Rita. It was almost funny. She had been given the job of following him. A very pleasant job, as far as Sarko was concerned. But now the job was over, and he would probably never see her again.

He sat up in his chair, not knowing which felt worse: feeling sorry for himself, or being angry at her.

He picked up the phone and dialed her number.

"Hello." It was her voice.

"I wasn't sure you'd still be at the same desk," he said, "now that your counterspy job is finished."

She laughed. "Hello, Paul. Frank told you about it, I see."

"Yes, Are you a full-time Intelligence operator, or do you just fill in during emergencies?"

"I'm a secretary," she said. "Frank noticed that we went out to lunch together a couple of times, so he asked me to keep an eye on you. For your own protection."

"You mean the first two times you went to lunch with me because . . ."

"Because I was hungry, and you asked me politely."

Sarko thought for a moment.

"It's just about lunchtime now," he said. "Are you hungry?"

"Starved."

"And how about dinner tonight?"

She said, "All right."

"And lunch tomorrow?"

"What is this?" Rita asked. "What are you up to, Paul?"

"I'm just trying to find out if you're as willing to go out with me now as you were when we still had a spy to catch."

Her voice grew serious. "I wasn't a very good counterspy, Paul. I was enjoying myself too much when I was with you."

Smiling, Sarko answered, "That makes two of us. I'll pick you up in ten minutes."

Late that night, long after dinner, Rita and Sarko were walking down a tree-lined street in the town next to the air base.

"Here's my house again," she said.

It was the fourth time they had walked past it.

"You're starting to sound sleepy," Sarko said. In the shadows cast by the trees, it was hard to see her face.

"A little," she admitted.

"There's something I've got to do," Sarko said abruptly. "I just realized it, just now. Something important."

"What's that?"

"I've got to go along with Frank when he flies Arrow Four to the Arctic."

"They won't let you, Paul. And why should you risk . . ."

"It's part of the job," he said firmly. "I can't just stop now. I've got to see this job through to the very end. No matter what."

CHAPTER FOURTEEN

Climbing at a steep angle toward 80,000 feet was like leaving the Earth and going into another world.

Sarko was sitting in a cockpit jammed with instruments. Dials and gauges and buttons and switches surrounded him. On his left sat Major Colt, in the pilot's seat. A set of throttles and engine control knobs separated the two seats.

Both men wore astronaut-type pressure suits and helmets. Hoses and wires connected them to the plane's oxygen, heating, and radio systems.

Colt eased up on the control wheel in front of him and Arrow Four leveled off. Sarko felt his back unglue itself from the back of his seat. There was almost no noise at all in the cockpit, except for some electrical humming and the whispering rush of air past the outer skin of the plane, just an inch over Sarko's head.

Both men wore specially-tinted visors over their eyes, to protect them from the flash of a laser's blinding light. The plane had been painted a gleaming white, to reflect the energy of the laser beam.

"I really feel like a knight in shining armor," Colt said with a grin.

With his right hand, he nudged the main throttle forward slightly, and the Mach meters on both cockpit control panels crept toward Mach 3.

"How do you like it?" the Major asked, turning to Sarko. The engineer heard his voice in his helmet earphones, over the Arrow's intercom radio.

"It's like coasting on a cloud . . . smoothest flight I've ever had."

Smiling, Colt said, "You deserve a smooth flight; you fought hard enough to get here."

"General Hastings wouldn't have let me come along if you hadn't helped to twist his arm."

"Well, I don't really need an electronics man for this run," Colt said. "We can use the ground radars to guide us, if we have to. Anyway, I have a feeling the other side will come looking for us. We won't have to go searching for him."

"That's why you're only using this one plane?"

Nodding, Colt answered, "Yeah. We don't want to scare 'em off."

"And what do you do when you come up against the enemy plane?"

"Swat the mosquito!" Colt snapped, fingering the trigger button on his control wheel.

The sky was an almost violet-blue above them, and far below the ground was covered with brilliant white clouds. They were miles above any weather.

Colt barely touched the controls. He kept the plane on the autopilot, and checked the radio now and then to make certain they were on the right course.

"You really think manned aircraft are going to be obsolete?" Colt asked.

It was difficult to nod inside the bulky flight helmet. Sarko turned to look at the Major, but his face was hidden behind the glare visor and oxygen mask.

"It's inevitable," Sarko answered. "Missiles have already made manned aircraft terribly vulnerable. Lasers—well, how are you going to dodge a weapon that strikes with the speed of light?"

Colt moved his shoulders in an exaggerated shrug. "Guess I'll have to move on, then."

"Out of the Air Force?"

"Hell no! I'm going to apply for astronaut training." He pointed a gloved finger straight up.

After about an hour's flying time, Sarko suddenly spotted another plane on the radar screen, far below them, outlined against the clouds.

He shook Colt's shoulder and pointed hurriedly.

The Major laughed. "It's our tanker. Good spotting."

They spiraled down as Colt identified himself on the radio to the waiting KC-135. The tanker let out its fuel line, and Colt deftly flew the Arrow's needle-tipped fuel probe straight into the connector.

The two planes linked, the connector locked, and fuel from the tanker began flowing into Arrow Four's hungry innards.

With all the fuel gauges reading full, Colt pulled Arrow Four free of the fuel line, wagged his wings in thanks, and pulled the control wheel back.

Sarko felt himself pressed against his seat again, as the Arrow climbed into the far sky.

"Next plane we see," Major Colt said quietly, "will be IT."

The clouds broke as they passed the northern edges of the Queen Elizabeth Islands and sailed out over the Arctic Ocean. Sarko could see ice floes among the deep swells of the ocean, but winter's broad icecap was gone.

"Might as well throw on your search radar." Colt pointed out the right switch. Sarko thumbed it, and a round screen on his instrument panel lighted up. A bright ray of light swept around it, like the second hand of a clock.

"I can keep an eye on it from here," the Major said. "You're supposed to be the missile-firing man on the team, as well as radio man, you know."

Sarko looked at him in surprise.

"Relax," Major Colt said. "We're not even carrying any missiles. Our official job is just to patrol the area and inspect any planes we can't identify. Inspect." He snorted.

"Then you're not supposed to shoot down the other plane."

"We're supposed to defend ourselves if we're attacked," Colt explained. "So we have a gun up in the nose. One gun. Fires, 6,000 rounds of 20-millimeter shells a minute. That's enough; we won't need any missiles."

"But if they don't attack us . . ."

"If they squirt that laser on us, it's an attack. And then we'll defend ourselves."

"But the laser won't hurt us!" Sarko said.

Colt's teeth flashed in a grin. "You know it won't hurt us, and I *think* it won't hurt us. But if they fire it, they're attacking us. And my orders give me a clear field to pump 6,000 rounds at 'em."

CHAPTER FIFTEEN

Sarko sank back in his seat.

"Arrow Four, this is station One-Oh-One. Do you read me?" Sarko heard the message crackle in his earphones.

"Got you, One-Oh-One," Colt said.

"We have a bogey at 75,000 feet. Moving southeast at about Mach 2. Shall we vector you in?"

"Yes," Colt answered eagerly. "Talk me in toward him."

He nosed the Arrow into the direction that the ground radar station gave him, and soon Sarko saw a little white blotch show up on the radar screen in front of him.

Closer and closer the radar pip came, in from the edge of the screen toward the middle.

Major Colt held the Arrow on a long, flat dive, throttled down to just about Mach 2.

"I see him!" he called out. "Visual contact."

Sarko looked in the direction of Colt's gaze and saw a tiny speck set against the sky. As they raced toward it, the speck grew and took shape: delta wings, four engines, and a big pod under the belly where the giant laser was housed.

Automatically, both men reached up and touched the special glare visors that covered their eyes, to make certain they were in place.

Sarko checked the special instruments that had been packed into his side of the cockpit; they would measure the enemy laser's power.

"They're coming at us dead-on," Colt muttered grimly. "Just like they did for the other three planes."

It seemed to Sarko as if they would have to crash. The two planes leaped at each other.

The special instruments beside him suddenly clicked.

"They fired the laser!" he shouted, looking down at the dials. "It hit us full blast!"

Just then Colt flipped the Arrow into a sharp right bank and turn, dangerously close to the other plane, and then it was out of sight.

"Okay, they attacked us," Colt said. "Now it's our turn."

He pulled the Arrow up, gained altitude, then circled to get behind the enemy bomber.

"But they didn't damage us. Their laser is useless now. It's finished as a weapon," Sarko, insisted.

Colt merely shook his head, like a man trying to get rid of an annoying insect.

Still holding the throttle down to the same speed as the enemy's, Colt edged up behind the bomber.

"No guns on him," he muttered. "Guess the laser equipment took up all the weight they could carry."

"They're defenseless."

"So were our guys . . . against their laser."

"But you can't just shoot them down in cold blood!"

"Can't I? Just watch."

Colt's thumb flicked the firing button, and Sarko felt the thunder and vibration of the gun.

"Just clearing the gun, making sure it's ready," the Major said softly. "Now . . . a little closer."

The bomber tried to twist and dodge, but Colt stayed right behind it and slightly to one side. He pulled the Arrow up so close that the bomber filled their vision, huge and black in front of them.

Colt's thumb hovered over the firing button.

"Don't do it, Frank!" Sarko begged. "Don't become just as bad as they are."

The Major glanced at Sarko. With a laugh, he flicked he hand from the red button to the main throttle.

Instead of firing, Colt gunned the Arrow's engines.

The plane zoomed past the surprised bomber and leaped high above the enemy.

Plastered into his seat, Sarko gasped, "What're you doing?"

"You don't want to kill 'em," Colt said. "But we've still got to show 'em we're better."

He made a wide swing around, then aimed the Arrow straight at the enemy bomber. They dived past the other plane, swung up again, and did a barrel roll completely around the bomber. Sarko felt his stomach trying to turn itself inside out.

Then Colt pulled up even with the enemy plane, waggled his wings, and did another roll, a full circle all around the bomber.

Sarko broke into a huge grin, despite his stomach. "I get it . . . you're flying rings around them!"

Colt nodded.

They pulled up even with the bomber again, close enough to see right into the enemy's cockpit. The copilot seemed to be yelling wildly into his radio mouthpiece; they could see his hands waving madly.

Colt raced ahead of the bomber, flew around it, over it, under it, sat off alongside one wing tip, then zipped over and parked near the other wing tip.

Finally the bomber turned and started back in the direction it had come from.

"They're going home," Sarko said.

Colt nodded. "And they won't be back again . . . not for a while, anyway. I think they got the message."

"You could have killed them, but you didn't."

"This was more fun. I'd just like to see the look on their generals' faces when they tell 'em what the Arrow can do."

"And tell them that the laser trick won't work anymore."

91

"Not that laser, anyway. They'll be back with something else, though, soon enough."

"And we'll be ready to counter them," Sarko said.

"What's this *we* stuff, white man? I'm going into the astronaut corps. Want to go into space with me?"

Grinning, Sarko said, "Sure. Why not?"

"You satisfied now? No blood spilled. Okay?"

"It was great, Frank. Simply great."

The Major laughed. "It was a lot better than shooting at 'em."

"Yes," Sarko agreed. "A lot better."

Colt nosed the Arrow into a long, graceful, sweeping turn and the two friends started for home.

THE FACTS ABOUT LASERS

Out of the Sun is fiction, but it is based on fact. In particular, it is based on the facts about one of the most remarkable inventions of the 20th century: the laser.

When I first wrote *Out of the Sun*, I had to check with friends of mine in the Air Force to make certain that I was not revealing any information about high-power lasers that the Defense Department had classified secret. At that time, I worked at Avco Everett Research Laboratory, where the very first truly high-power lasers had been developed. The laser used as a weapon in the novel you have just read was actually not as powerful or efficient as lasers that were then being developed in the laboratory!

The pages to come will show how lasers were first dreamed about, then invented, and then developed into important tools for both military and civilian applications. As you will see, lasers have left the realm of science fiction and are now "front page news."

THE AMAZING LASER

THE AMAZING LASER

Is Dedicated To

DR. I. M. LEVITT

who started this book
some thirty-five years ago
without knowing it.

Codes and Guides

Here are some aids to help you explore the amazing world of the laser.

THE METRIC SYSTEM

World scientists now use the metric system rather than the older and clumsier English system of inches, pounds, and so forth.

LENGTH

1 millimeter (mm) = 0.03937 inch
1 centimeter (cm) = 0.3937 inch
1 meter (m) = 100 cm = 39.37 inches, or 3.28 feet
1 kilometer (km) = 1000 m = 0.62137 mile
1 mile = 1.6093 km
1 inch = 2.5400 cm = 25.400 mm

WEIGHT

1 gram (gm) = 0.0353 ounce = 0.0022046 pound
1 kilogram (kg) = 1000 gm = 2.2046 pounds
1 metric ton = 1000 kg = 2204.6 pounds

TEMPERATURE SCALES

Three temperature scales are in common use today. The Kelvin, or Absolute, scale is used most in this book. The Kelvin scale starts at absolute zero, the temperature where, theoretically, all molecular motion stops and the energy we call heat ceases to exist. There are no minus numbers in the Kelvin scale.

The centigrade scale uses the same "sized" degrees as the Kelvin. The only difference between the two scales is that the centigrade scale places its zero at the freezing point of fresh water. In converting from centigrade to Kelvin, merely add 273; to go from Kelvin to centigrade, subtract 273. The Fahrenheit scale is older and much different. To convert from centigrade degrees to Fahrenheit, multiply by 9/5 and then add 32. To go from Fahrenheit to centigrade, subtract 32 and then multiply by 5/9.

	Degrees Kelvin	Degrees Centigrade	Degrees Fahrenheit
Water boils	373	100	212
Water freezes	273	0	32
Absolute zero	0	−273	−459

NAMES FOR LARGE AND SMALL UNITS

Such terms as megawatts and kilovolts are simple ways of labeling even units. Prefixes that denote large and small units include:

tera = 10^{12}	deci = 10^{-1}
giga = 10^9	centi = 10^{-2}
mega = 10^6	milli = 10^{-3}
kilo = 10^3	micro = 10^{-6}
hecto = 10^2	nano = 10^{-9}
deka = 10	pico = 10^{-12}

POWERS OF TEN

In writing very large or very small numbers, the powers of ten notation saves work and space.

$10 = 10^1$	$1 = 10^0$
$100 = 10^2$	$0.1 = 10^{-1}$
$1000 = 10^3$	$0.01 = 10^{-2}$
$1,000,000 = 10^6$	$0.000001 = 10^{-6}$
$1,000,000,000 = 10^9$	$0.000000001 = 10^{-9}$

A *plus* superscript tells how many zeroes are to the left of the decimal place, and a *minus* superscript tells how many digits (not only zeroes) are to the right of the decimal. To write out a number such as 83 billion we say:

$$83 \times 10^9 \text{ or } 8.3 \times 10^{10}$$

1
Science Fiction Comes True

Suddenly there was a flash of light. . . . At the same time a faint hissing sound became audible. . . . Forthwith flashes of actual flame, a bright glare . . . sprang from the group of men. It was as if some invisible jet impinged upon them and flashed into white flame. It was as if each man were suddenly and momentarily turned to fire. . . . It was sweeping round swiftly and steadily, this flaming death, this invisible, inevitable sword of heat.

That is how H. G. Wells described the "heat ray" weapon used by Martians against Earthmen in his book *The War of the Worlds*, published in 1898.

On January 12, 1970, the magazine *Aviation Week* carried a story about lasers that said:

> These radiation weapons, or "death rays," an enticing topic of science fiction . . . could have a resounding impact on the conduct of modern warfare. . . . This follows the successful shooting down of a drone aircraft with a laser.

Over the next dozen years military scientists have continued to develop laser weaponry. In 1983 the Air Force announced that several heat-seeking Sidewinder missiles had been shot down by a 400-kilowatt laser flown aboard the Airborne Laser Laboratory, in a test in California. An even more powerful laser, capable of power outputs of more than a megawatt (one million watts) is being tested at the White Sands Proving Grounds, in New Mexico.

You probably know that the laser is a device that produces light—extremely intense, brilliant light, brighter than the sun.

Laser beams are so intense that they've been bounced off the Moon and detected back here on Earth. The lasers that were used to do this produced only a few watts of light power. Yet their light was bright enough to be seen after a round-trip journey of some 760,000 kilometers. Could the light from a 50-watt lamp travel to the Moon and back and still be bright enough to be seen?

The first successful laser was made in 1960. Within ten years, lasers had become powerful enough to be considered as weapons of war.

It would be terribly discouraging to think that this bright new invention would find its main use as a military weapon. Mankind has a long and unhappy history of turning brilliant ideas into new ways of fighting. The wheel was invented some 10,000 years ago and promptly used to make war chariots. Iron and steel were turned into swords and armor. Airplanes and submarines have carried war into the clouds and the depths of the sea. Nuclear power brought A-bombs and H-bombs. Rockets have been turned into globe-spanning missiles.

Yet, on the other hand, all these inventions have also helped to make civilization strong and life more fruitful. Where would we be today without wheels, or steel, or airplanes? The electricity that lights your home might well be produced by a nuclear power station. And rockets carry men to the Moon, orbit satellites that watch our weather, and relay television and telephone signals around the world.

Any invention, any idea, can be used for many different purposes. Sometimes these purposes are military, for war. More often they are peaceful and very helpful to mankind.

So it is with lasers.

Lasers are being used today by medical researchers for many things, from attacking cancer cells to erasing tattoos.

Lasers are being used for communications. Laser beams have carried television broadcasts for many kilometers. When men travel to Mars, they will probably use a powerful laser to send live television broad-

NATIONAL NEWSPAPER SYNDICATE, INC.

casts to Earth from more than 100 million kilometers' distance.

Lasers are already at work in factories, where they are used for welding, cutting, measuring, and other tasks. Computer engineers are starting to use lasers to help build new types of computers that will be smaller and work faster than today's models. Lasers guide huge tunneling machines, where their beams of light keep the machines going precisely in a straight line.

And lasers have produced an exciting new possibility of making three-dimensional pictures, called *holograms*. In a holographic picture, the objects in the picture appear to be actually standing in front of you. If you move your head, you can see behind the objects!

Most important of all, perhaps, is the fact that scientists and engineers are just beginning to develop the uses of lasers. Lasers are so new and so different from any other type of light source that they've often been called "a solution in search of a problem." That is, lasers offer a brilliant new opportunity to do new things in science, engineering, medicine, industry, and many other fields.

The real problem now is to find out what jobs the laser does best. Most likely, the laser will allow us to do things that we never thought of doing before!

Lasers are being used in scientific research as a tool that allows very precise measurements to be made, as a means of producing three-dimensional holograms during an experiment, and as a means of studying the properties of light itself. Out of this research comes a better understanding of the world around us. And from such understanding come new ideas, new ways of life. The laser itself is the result of such research, as we'll see in the next few chapters.

WHAT IS A LASER?

So far we have been talking about lasers without saying exactly what a laser is or how it differs from other sources of light, such as a candle or a flashlight.

The word "laser" is an *acronym*. That is, it's a word made by putting together the initial letters of other words. In this case, the other words are

Light

Amplification by

Stimulated

Emission of

Radiation

Like most definitions, that one raises more questions than it answers. We'll look more deeply into what those words mean in the following chapters. For now, let's focus our attention on the way that a laser is different from other light sources.

There are four main differences between lasers and all other sources of light, such as lamps, flames, stars, and so on. Laser light is more intense, it comes out in a narrow beam, it it monochromatic (one color), and it is coherent. To explain:

Intensity. The light produced by a laser can be made fantastically intense, much brighter than the light given off by the sun. The sun emits about 7,000 watts (7 kilowatts) of light energy from each square centimeter of its surface. That's equal to the energy from seventy 100-watt light bulbs, coming out of an area about the size of a postage stamp!

Lasers have produced brusts of light that have more than a *billion* watts of energy in a beam about 1 square centimeter in cross section. That's a gigawatt, or a million kilowatts. And laser beams have been focused down to tiny spots where their concentrated energy has amounted to more than 10 gigawatts per square centimeter.

Of course, the sun is huge: about a million kilometers in diameter. It emits a tremendous amount of total energy. But lasers are brighter! They put out more energy per square centimeter than the sun does.

This means that lasers can be extremely dangerous to your eyes. You should never look directly at a laser beam unless you're wearing special protective goggles. And *no one* ever looks straight into a laser, even with safety goggles, any more than a sane person squints down the barrel of a gun.

Directionality. Lasers can be made to emit very narrow, pencil-thin beams of light. Their beams spread very little.

How many times have you taken a flashlight out

LIGHT BULB

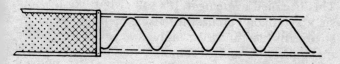

LASER

Waves from a light bulb are jumbled. Waves from a laser are precisely spaced and directed.

on a dark evening and aimed it at a distant target? How far does the beam go before fading into dimness?

Yet rather low-powered lasers, which put out only a few watts of light energy, have bounced their beams off the Moon. They could do this partly because the laser beam is so narrow and doesn't spread very much. The beam can carry much farther, since it doesn't waste its energy by spreading out widely. The laser beams that have reached the Moon have spread to a diameter of only a few kilometers, after a trip of some 380,000 kilometers.

Monochromaticity. "Monochromatic" is a big word that means "one color."

An ordinary source of light, such as the lamp you are reading by, or the sun if you are out of doors, emits light of many different colors, all mixed together. This is called *white light*. It's somewhat like the music a symphony orchestra makes, many different instruments blending their individual voices to produce the orchestra's unified sound. Actually, white light is more like the noise the orchestra is making when the players are tuning up!

The light that the laser emits is more like the voice of a single violin than the sound of a whole orchestra. A laser's light is one color and usually a very pure color too.

There are many different types of lasers, and laser beams have been produced in every color of the rainbow. Lasers even produce forms of light that the human eye can't see—infrared (IR) and ultraviolet (UV) radiation.

Some lasers can be made to produce more than

one color by changing the way the laser is operated. There are lasers that can be "tuned" to produce any color you want, from deepest red to deepest violet. Such "tunable" lasers are rather like a violin that can produce a wide variety of musical notes—but only one note at a time. The beam coming from a tunable laser is always monochromatic, one color. You can change the color though.

Coherence. Laser light is coherent. That is, the waves of light coming out of a laser are all lined up together, precisely in step.

Picture in your mind the surf rolling up on a beach. The waves curling in are each different. Some are big, steep waves. Some are little ripples. Sometimes they come closely spaced together, one wave after another. Other times there is a long wait between one wave and the next.

Now imagine, if you can, a beach where all the waves are exactly alike: all the same height, all the same direction, always the same spacing between them. That's how the light waves from a laser are.

Ordinary light sources produce light waves of many different types, all jumbled together, like an auditorium full of freewheeling rock dancers. Lasers produce light waves that are more precisely spaced and lined up than a marching squad of West Point cadets. This quality of laser light is called coherence, and laser light is said to be coherent.

We can see now that lasers produce light of unequaled intensity, light beams that are highly directional, and light that is monochromatic and coherent.

But we don't know yet what happens inside a laser to make these special qualities come out. To understand that, we must first find out a few things about this rather mysterious thing called *light*.

2
Light: Particles or Waves?

WHAT IS LIGHT?

This simple question has led scientists on a hectic chase for more than 300 years. Much of the study of physics depends on understanding what *energy* is, and light is a form of pure energy. Since the beginnings of modern physics in the seventeenth century, men of science have tried to understand the nature of light. Their studies have led to the laser.

What can we find out about the nature of light? We can start by asking ourselves how light travels. It seems clear that light comes from sources such as lamps or flames. How does it go from a source to our eyes?

Get a model airplane or some other object and stand it in front of a white background. A wall, a bed sheet, or a movie screen will do perfectly well. Now shine a flashlight on the model and turn out all the other lights in the room. The flashlight casts a shadow of the model on the background screen or wall. By moving the light source to the proper distance away from the model, you can make the shadow on the wall quite sharp.

Now ask yourself, How does the light travel from the source to the wall? Get a long string and tape it to one particular point on the shadow—say, the tip of one wing. Now connect the string to the wing of the model and tape it in place. Finally, connect the string from the model's wing tip to the flashlight itself.

You'll see that the string forms one continuous straight line, from the light source to the model to the shadow. Light apparently moves in straight lines.

When you turn on the flashlight, the screen is lighted up instantly, and the shadow appears. Does the light cross the distance to the screen instantly, or does it take some time to get there? How fast does light travel?

THE SPEED OF LIGHT

Galileo Galilei (1564–1642) asked himself that same question. Galileo was the first truly modern scientist.

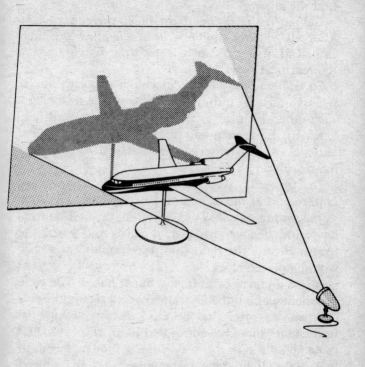

Rays of light go in a straight line from the lamp to the screen, outlining the plane.

He didn't merely wonder about a problem, or argue about it. He tried experiments and measurements to find the answer.

Galileo realized that light must travel very fast. After all, when a candle is lit at the altar of a huge cathedral, its light can be seen immediately even at the rearmost pews.

So Galileo designed an ingenious experiment. He put two men on hilltops, a long distance away from each other. He measured the distance between them carefully. Each man had a lantern, and one of them had a clock. The lanterns were shielded, so that their light couldn't be seen.

The first man would drop the shielding from his lantern and at the same time start his clock. As soon as the second man saw the light from the first lantern, he would uncover his own lantern. And when the first man saw the light from the second lantern, he would stop the clock.

It was a clever experiment, but it failed. The time between opening the first lantern and seeing the second was so brief that no clock could measure it! Galileo was forced to admit that light travels too fast to be measured in this way. Others, though, began to believe that light moves instantaneously, and its speed is impossible to measure by any means because its speed is infinite.

It wasn't until 1676 that the Danish astronomer Ole Roemer (1644–1710) showed that light isn't instantaneous, although its speed is fantastically high. Interestingly, Roemer's measurement of the speed of

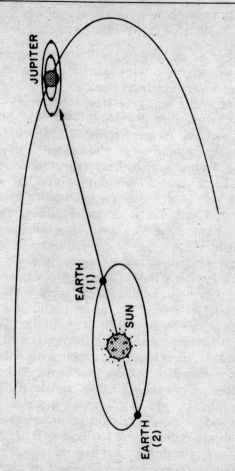

By timing the eclipses of Jupiter's moons from (1) and (2),
Roemer measured the time it took light to travel across the
earth's orbit and calculated the speed of light

light was based on one of Galileo's most striking discoveries.

In 1609 Galileo became the first astronomer to use a telescope. With a telescope he built himself, the Italian genius made many startling discoveries which shook the whole European intellectual world. One of his most astounding observations was that the planet Jupiter had four moons circling it. In those days, the Earth was thought to be the center of the whole universe. To find four bodies circling another planet, not the Earth, was dramatic proof that our world is not the hub of the universe. Today we know that Jupiter has at least a dozen satellites, but with Galileo's pioneering telescope, only the brightest four were visible.

By Roemer's time, nearly seventy years later, the orbits of Jupiter's moons had been calculated well enough that astronomers could predict with good accuracy when each of the moons would pass behind Jupiter's huge bulk and be eclipsed by the giant planet. Roemer reasoned that there was a "lantern" that could be used to measure the speed of light.

Roemer found that when our own planet Earth was in the part of its orbit that brought it closest to Jupiter, the eclipse of a Jovian moon happened about 11 minutes earlier than predicted. And when the Earth and Jupiter were farthest apart, the eclipses came some 11 minutes late. Roemer concluded that the 11-minute differences were actually measurements of the time it took light to cross the Earth's orbit. The "early" eclipses were due to the fact that the Earth was close enough to receive the light from

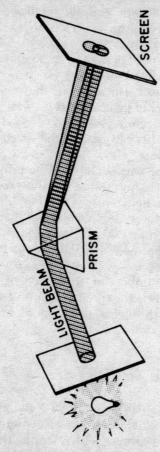

Different wavelengths of light travel through glass at different speeds and emerge from a prism at different angles, so
that colors are separated

119

distant Jupiter and its moons sooner than the calculations predicted. The "late" eclipses happened because the light had to travel an extra distance, since the Earth was farther away.

To calculate the speed of light, then, Roemer needed only to know the diameter of the Earth's orbit and divide by 22 minutes. However, in the seventeenth century the diameter of the Earth's orbit wasn't known to any reasonable accuracy, and Roemer's clock was inaccurate too. So his estimate of the speed of light was not very accurate.

But his technique was sound, and he proved that light does travel at a finite—not infinite—speed. Today we know that light crosses the Earth's orbital diameter in 16 minutes, 36 seconds, and that diameter is slightly less than 300 million kilometers long. The speed of light has been calculated to be 299,792.5 kilometers per second.

A good round number for the speed of light is 300,000 km/sec. This is the speed of light in a vacuum. When light passes through a gas, a liquid, or a solid, its speed is slowed down.

THE PARTICLE THEORY

The year that Galileo died, Isaac Newton (1642–1727) was born in England. It was Newton who began to study light in earnest, with scientific thoroughness. His great book *Optiks* was published in 1704; it laid the foundation for our modern understanding of light.

Curiously, Newton shied away from trying to explain what light is—and for good reason, as we'll soon see. In *Optiks* he explained much of the way light behaves, and explained it so well that his ideas are still used today to make lenses and mirrors.

For example, he showed why sunlight is broken up into a rainbow of colors when it passes through a glass prism. Newton deduced that sunlight consists of different colors, which we see all mixed together as white light. When white light goes through a prism, the glass material slows down some of the colors more than others. The result is that each individual color comes out of the prism at a slightly different angle, and the light is spread into a gleaming rainbow. The droplets of water in a rain shower act as natural prisms to produce the beautiful arch of the rainbow on a sunny-showery day.

The scientific name for this glowing band of colors is *spectrum*. There will be more on the spectrum later.

Newton's only attempt to explain the basic nature of light was little more than his own opinion, without much scientific evidence to back it up. He believed that light was made up of a stream of tiny particles, almost like microscopic bullets. He believed that these particles of light traveled at enormous velocity from a light source such as a flame or a star. He based his belief in this particle theory of light mainly on the grounds that light travels in straight lines. The simplest explanation for straight-line travel, Newton thought, was that light consists of tiny streams of particles.

121

But before Newton's *Optiks*, the Dutch scientist Christiaan Huygens (1629–1695) had suggested that light was actually a wave motion, not particles. He pictured light waves that come from a candle, for example, much in the same way that ripples spread across a pond when a pebble is dropped into the water. But water waves are limited to the surface of the water and make two-dimensional circles. Light waves move in three dimensions, making growing spheres, rather like ever-expanding balloons.

Huygens was a famous and respected scientist. Like Newton, he was interested in optics and telescopes; he discovered that the planet Saturn has rings around it and made many other contributions to astronomy, mathematics, and physics.

But whereas Huygens was a giant, Newton was a supergiant. His work in optics was only one small part of the enormous contributions he made to physics and mathematics. His most famous work dealt with the basic laws of motion and gravity. So it was Newton's opinion that carried the most weight among scientists. For almost a century, Newton's particle theory held sway over Huygens' wave theory of light. It might seem strange that scientists can be swayed by opinions, but remember that there was little evidence to decide the issue either way. When the evidence is scanty, opinions and reputations hold the field. And Newton's reputation—even today—is among the highest in all of science.

THE WAVE THEORY

Newton himself realized that there were certain things about the behavior of light that couldn't be easily explained by the particle theory. But, as so often happens in human affairs, Newton's followers backed the particle theory even more strongly than he did. It wasn't until early in the nineteenth century that experiments by Thomas Young (1773–1829) in England and the French physicist Augustin Jean Fresnel (1788–1827) shattered the particle theory and established the wave theory as the most satisfactory explanation for the nature of light.

Young was a physician, a medical doctor, as well as a physicist. His interest in light and optics stemmed mainly from his curiosity about the way the human eye works. He developed a theory that attempted to explain how we see colors. But his most important contribution to our understanding of light came in an experiment that he performed in 1803. You can do the same experiment and duplicate his results.

You need three screens—white cardboard will do—a source of light such as a flashlight or small lamp, and a pin.

Start with two of the screens. Place the lamp on one side of the first screen, close enough so that the screen blocks all its light. Now put the second screen a meter or so farther away. Then carefully make the tiniest pinhole you can in the first screen, at its center.

Light waves filtered by pinholes in screens create interference patterns like ripples in a pool

If all the lights in the room are off, except for the lamp, you'll see the second screen illuminated only by the light coming through the pinhole. It's rather dimly lit, but the light should be evenly distributed across the entire screen.

Now take the third screen and put two tiny pinholes in it, then place this new screen between the first two. The light now travels from the lamp, through the single hole of the first screen, through the two holes of the middle screen, and onto the farthest screen. What happens at the farthest screen?

The light is no longer spread evenly across the screen! There's a checkerboard pattern of bright spots and dark spots. How can this be?

If your school has a ripple tank in its science lab, you can use it to understand what's happening. A ripple tank is simply a shallow tank of water, with two little prongs that can be rapidly dipped into the water to make circular waves.

When the mechanical prongs, or "fingers," are both making waves at the same time, you can see a pattern of bright and dark spots on the lighted bottom of the tank. This pattern will look very much like the pattern in our duplication of Young's experiment, and for good reason: exactly the same thing is happening.

Waves have certain things in common, whether they're water waves or light waves. A wave has a certain height, which is measured from its *crest* (highest point) to its *trough* (lowest point). Waves also come in various lengths, as measured from crest to crest (or trough to trough if you want to). Not

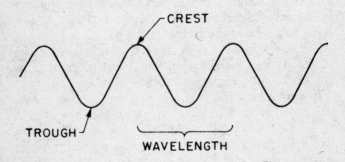

surprisingly, this is called the *wavelength*. And waves also have a *frequency*, which is simply the number of waves that pass a fixed point within a certain amount of time, usually one second. Incidentally, the height of a wave is generally called its *amplitude*.

Now then, in the ripple tank we set two patterns of waves against each other. The growing circles of waves made by one mechanical finger run into the circular waves coming from the other finger. When the two sets of waves meet, they interfere with each other.

If two waves happen to come together when they are both at crest, they *reinforce* each other to make an extra-high wave. This is called *positive interference*. If they come together where they are both at trough, they reinforce also, and make an extra-deep trough. If the crest of one wave meets the trough of another, they simply *cancel* each other. That's called *negative interference*.

So the pattern of water waves in the ripple tank and the pattern of light waves in Young's experiment are caused by interference. The two pinholes act somewhat like the two ripple-making fingers in the water tank.

If light behaved like a stream of bullets, Young's experiment wouldn't have produced interference patterns. Can you figure out for yourself what Young's experiment would have looked like if light actually did behave like bullets?

Young's experiment, and other work by Fresnel and many other researchers, showed that light behaves in a way that Newton's particle theory simply can't expalin. The wave theory of light won a complete victory—even though it was really not correct.

3
Photons and "Wavicles"

It wasn't until the twentieth century that a new understanding of light replaced the wave theory. But the wave theory was extremely valuable. It explained not only light but many other things as well.

During the first half of the nineteenth century, scientists began to understand the nature of electricity and magnetism. The Danish physicist and chemist Hans Christian Oersted (1777–1851) showed that electricity and magnetism were always linked together. Today, as a result of the work that Oersted pioneered, we speak of *electromagnetic forces*. In England, Michael Faraday (1791–1867) discovered a way to gener-

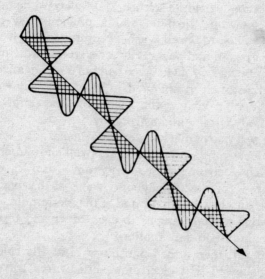

All electromagnetic waves have electrical and magnetic
components that vibrate at right angles to each other

ate electrical power. His primitive "dynamos" were the forerunners of the electrical generators and motors that run so much of our modern civilization.

Then came James Clerk Maxwell (1831–1879), the brilliant Scottish scientist. For sheer genius and impact of many fields of science, Maxwell must be ranked with Newton, Einstein, and a precious few other supergiants. Maxwell was a theoretician; he worked with a pencil and paper. His tools were mathematics and his work brought about important advances in the areas of electromagnetism, light, the behavior of gases, color vision, the study of heat known as thermodynamics, and astronomy.

He was particularly interested in Faraday's work with electromagnetic forces. Maxwell showed on paper that electromagnetic energy moves as a wave. He pictured the electromagnetic wave as having two parts: an electrical field and a magnetic field, both vibrating at right angles to each other and to their common direction of motion.

Maxwell then added one more idea. His calculations showed that electromagnetic waves travel at the same speed as light waves. So he concluded—on this basis alone—that light and electromagnetic waves are actually the same. Light is a particular kind of electromagnetic wave.

He had no experimental evidence for this conclusion, merely his own hunch. The history of science is dotted with cases in which a man makes a leap into the unknown based on little more than his own intuition. Many of the great strides forward in science started as little more than hunches. So did many of the wrong guesses.

Maxwell pictured electromagnetism as an enormous spectrum of waves, waves of pure energy. Visible light is only one small slice of the electromagnetic spectrum, he reasoned. If this is true, his fellow scientists asked, then where are the other types of electromagnetic waves that are invisible to us? Can they be found? And used?

Not until nine years after Maxwell's death was the first of these "invisible waves" found. In 1888 the young German physicist Henrich Hertz (1857–1894) set up a simple experiment. His equipment produced an electrical spark between two metal balls. The spark was made to crackle back and forth in the tiny gap between the balls. Maxwell's equations had predicted that such a spark should emit invisible electromagnetic waves. Across his room from the spark source, Hertz set up a simple loop of wire, with a gap in it of the same size as the spark gap.

When he allowed electrical current to flow into the metal balls and cause the spark to flash, a similar spark immediately sprang up in the wire loop across the room. Hertz had proved that invisible electromagnetic waves can travel over a distance from a *transmitter* of electromagnetic energy to a *receiver*, without any wires or other man-made connection.

The waves were immediately called "Hertzian waves" and stirred up tremendous enthusiasm among scientists and engineers—for Hertz had built the first radio.

Seven years later, in 1895, Wilhelm Roentgen

(1845–1923), of Germany, discovered a very different kind of electromagnetic radiation. These waves came from heavy elements such as radium and uranium, and they could go through solid matter as easily as light goes through glass. Originally called "Roentgen rays," they're now known by the name that the puzzled Roentgen himself gave to them: *X-rays.*

Today we know that the electromagnetic spectrum extends from radio waves that are many kilometers long down to waves that are so small that a hundred billion of them can be packed into a meter's length.

We use many parts of the long side of the electromagnetic spectrum for radio, television, radar, and even radio astronomy. Just outside the visible spectrum there are the infrared rays, which we use in heat lamps. On the short-wavelength side of the visible spectrum are the ultraviolet rays, which give us a suntan (or a burn if we're careless). Shorter still are the X-rays, which are useful in medical examinations of our bodies' insides, and finally the gamma rays.

WHEN IS A WAVE NOT A WAVE?

Hertz died at the age of thirty-seven, but during his tragically brief lifetime he made another important discovery about light and energy.

In 1889, during the course of his many experiments, he found that if he placed a sheet of glass between the spark transmitter and the receiver, the spark in the receiver's gap became much weaker. Puzzling

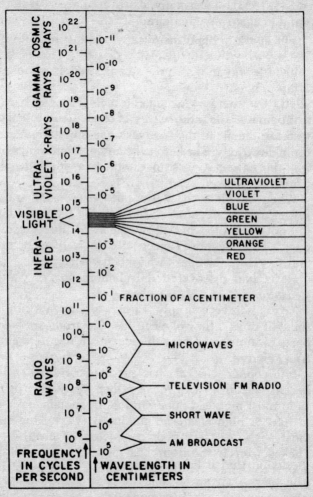

The electromagnetic spectrum

over this, Hertz came to a rather complicated explanation of what was going on.

The spark in his transmitter was emitting not only radio waves but ultraviolet waves too. This is very much the way in which the steady spark in a tanning lamp puts out UV energy.

The UV energy reached the receiver's gap at the same time as the radio waves, of course. And it helped to make the air in the receiver's gap a better conductor of electricity. The better the air conducted electricity, the easier it was to establish a spark in the transmitter's gap.

When the glass sheet was put between the transmitter and the receiver, it blocked the UV radiation, but not the radio waves. Now the air in the receiver's gap couldn't conduct electricity so well as before, and therefore the spark was much weaker.

Hertz had discovered the phenomenon of *photoionization*.

To explain very simply: Electrical currents can be thought of as a flow of electrons. Electrons are basic parts of atoms, the part that carries a negative electrical charge.

In a copper wire, electric currents can flow easily because electrons can move rather freely in copper, as in most metals. Copper and many metals are said to have a high electrical conductivity. But air and most gases are very poor conductors of electricity. The electrons in the atoms of a gas tend to be strongly bound to the atoms; they don't move away from the atoms very easily. It takes a lot of energy to tear them loose and to free enough electrons so that the gas will conduct electricity reasonably well. This process of freeing electrons from their parent atoms is called *ionization*.

The ultraviolet energy coming from Hertz's transmitter somehow wrenched electrons free from the atoms in the air at the receiver, and so made the air a better electrical conductor. When atoms are ionized by light, or even UV "light," the process is called photoionization, "photo" coming from the Greek word for light.

How can electromagnetic waves tear electrons loose from atoms?

PACKAGES OF LIGHT

The discovery of photoionization was not only the first step in our modern understanding of light, but it also began an upheaval that transformed all of physics.

The next link in the chain came from an unexpected direction. The German physicist Max Planck (1858–1947) was trying to solve some fundamental problems in the field of thermodynamics, which is the study of heat and energy. The details of his work do not concern us now. What is important is that in 1900 Planck came to the conclusion that energy exists in distinct packets, which he called *quanta* (singular, *quantum*).

Planck's *quantum theory* was another bold leap forward that was backed by little more than a single man's intuition. Many physicists rejected the quantum theory right away. After all, Planck seemed to be trying to revive the old particle theory of light under a fancier name—but only at first glance. His quanta weren't like Newton's microscopic bullets of light. Energy quanta still showed all the properties of electromagnetic waves. But, in addition, they could also behave like particles!

It was hard to accept the idea that light or other forms of electromagnetic energy could be *both* particles and waves, but Planck's work started a revolution in physics such as hadn't been seen since the time of Galileo and Newton. Man's entire concept of the nature of the physical world underwent a complete change, thanks to the work of Planck and those who followed him. Planck received the Nobel Prize in 1918 for his development of the quantum theory.

One of the brilliant men who helped to carry on this revolution in physics was Albert Einsten (1879–1955). In 1905, while a clerk in the Swiss Patent Office, Einstein brought together Hertz's photoionization work and Planck's quantum theory. The result is called the *photoelectric effect*. It was the next step forward in man's understanding light and energy.

Einstein was intrigued by experiments in which plates of zinc were illuminated by light. In these experiments, when the light struck the metal, electrons were freed from the metal. You would expect that the stronger the light, the faster and more energetic the electrons would be.

But this wasn't the case at all. Making the light more intense—that is, showering more energy on the metal—did not produce more-energetic electrons. The electrons that came off the zinc had the same velocity as those produced by less-intense light. The stronger light produced more electrons, but not more-energetic electrons.

More-energetic electrons *were* produced, though, when light of shorter wavelengths was used. Blue light yielded more-energetic electrons than red light. And ultraviolet light brought the electrons out of the zinc at even higher speeds.

Why?

Working with pencil and paper, Einstein tried to solve this riddle. He knew of Planck's quantum theory and applied it to this problem. Suppose each quantum of light had a certain amount of energy associated with it. And suppose there is more energy per quantum for shorter wavelengths than for longer. Einstein found he could use Planck's mathematics to help solve the problem of the photoelectric effect. He showed that the energy in a quantum of light was directly related to the energy that the electron had when it came off the zinc.

In brief, the light quanta were knocking electrons out of the zinc atoms, and the electrons came away with just the same amount of energy that the light quanta had in the first place.

Einstein published his work on the photoelectric effect in 1905, the same year that he published his first paper on his theory of relativity. In 1921 he was awarded the Nobel Prize for this work on the photoelectric effect.

INTO THE ATOM

It now seemed clear that light was definitely more than just an electromagnetic wave. The wave theory could not explain the photoelectric effect nor many other things about the behavior of light.

Physicists began to call the basic quantum of light the *photon*. Some aspects of the photon's behavior were best described by thinking of it as a wave. Other aspects were best described as actions of a particle. Half jokingly, a few scientists began to call the photon a *wavicle*.

It's a bit strange to think of the photon as both a particle and a wave. Yet this description best fits all the things that have been observed about light's behavior. Photons are certainly not particles in the same sense that Newton's "bullets" were particles.

Whether it is described as a particle of a wave, each photon has a certain definite amount of energy— no more and no less. This is usually called the *quantum energy* of the photon, and the shorter the wavelength of a photon, the more quantum energy it contains. This is why UV photons produced more-energetic electrons than did visible photons.

In 1913 the Danish physicist Niels Bohr (1885–1962) provided a basic explanation for the way that light and atoms interact. His work paved the way for understanding how atoms produce photons and why the quantum theory correctly explains the nature of light.

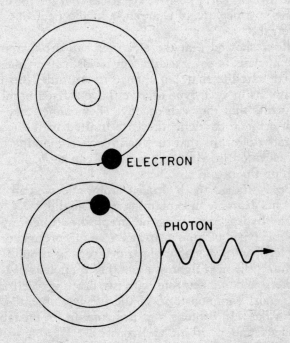

When the electron drops from one level to another, energy is released.

By this time, physicists understood that the atom consisted of a dense nucleus made up of protons and neutrons, with electrons orbiting around this nucleus. The protons carry positive electrical charges, the electrons are negatively charged, and the neutrons are neutral.

Bohr showed that the electrons can orbit around the nucleus at several different levels, rather like an Earth satellite that can change its altitude. But the electrons in each type of atom have a fixed number of orbits that they can occupy. They cannot take up any orbit at random; they are limited in the exact number of orbits that they can reach, something like an elevator in a skyscraper that can stop only at certain floors and no others.

Bohr studied the hydrogen atom, and we can follow his example in explaining what he did.

The hydrogen atom is the simplest and lightest of all the types of atoms. It has a single proton for a nucleus, with a single electron orbiting around it. Helium, the next lightest atom, has a nucleus of two protons and two neutrons with two orbiting electrons. The most common form of the heavy element uranium has 238 protons and neutrons in its unstable nucleus, and 92 orbital electrons.

Bohr found that the lone electron of the hydrogen atom can jump to several different orbits, depending on the energy level of the atom. When the electron is in its lowest possible orbit, this is the lowest energy level, and the electron and atom are said to be in the *rest state*. But if a quantum of energy—a photon— reaches the atom, it can stimulate the electron to move into a higher orbit. The atom is then said to be in an *excited state*. Excitement of any kind never lasts long, though, and the electron tends to jump back down to as low an orbit as possible. When the electron hops down from a high-energy excited state to a lower-energy orbit, it gives off a photon.

And all this happens in quanta.

The electron will not move from its orbit unless it receivers exactly the right quantum of energy—exactly the right quantum, no more and no less.

Picture a hydrogen atom in the rest state. Its electron is orbiting as close to the nucleus as possible. This is the most stable condition. Photons of various quantum energies (or wavelengths) come by, but the atom is unaffected by them because they are not the proper quantum energy to affect the electron.

Then along comes a photon with a quantum energy that matches the energy needed to boost the electron to a higher orbit. The electron absorbs this energy, the photon disappears, and the electron jumps to the higher orbit. The excited state isn't really stable, however, so the electron rather quickly hops back down to its original rest-state orbit. When it comes down, it gives up the extra energy it had absorbed. It gives off a photon—a photon of exactly the same quantum energy, or wavelength, as the photon it had originally absorbed.

The hydrogen atom can absorb photons of several different wavelengths—but only those wavelengths. The situation is something like a candy-vending machine. If you put in a coin that's too small or too large, you get nothing. You must put in just the right-sized coin to get what you want.

And when the atom releases a photon, it can only be a photon of a certain fixed set of wavelengths. Thus, physicists and chemists can tell what types of atoms—what elements—are present in a material by making the material give off light. This field of science is called *spectroscopy*, and it's rather like identifying a person by his fingerprints: atoms can be identified by the wavelengths of the photons they emit.

QUANTUM MECHANICS

Bohr showed the atom to be a dynamic thing, with the electrons constantly hopping back and forth from one orbit to another, absorbing photons or emitting them. His followers carried his work on to the other elements, with their heavier, more complex atoms. Bohr received the Nobel Prize in 1922 for this work.

In the meantime, all of physics was being revolutionized. Men such as Louis de Broglie (born 1892) in France, the German Werner Heisenberg (1901–1976), and Austrian Erwin Schrödinger (1887–1961) built the foundations of *quantum mechanics*, a new view of how the physical universe works. In 1916 Einstein published his general theory of relativity, which tied together much of this new understanding of nature.

Very simply, quantum mechanics and general relativity pointed out that matter and energy are one and the same thing. Not only is light a "wavicle," but all matter and energy are wavicles. Einstein's famous equation, $E = mc^2$, shows the relationship between the mass of a bit of matter and the energy it contains.

Light, energy, and solid matter are merely different forms of the same thing. Mass is energy and energy is mass. This sheet of paper is composed of wavicles of matter which can be thought of as "frozen energy."

The new physics of quantum mechanics and relativity didn't overthrow the older physics. Newton, Young, Maxwell, and the other physicists who came before the twentieth century weren't wrong. The new physics builds on their foundations and goes farther than they could go. It explains more about the universe than Newtonian physics could.

The English physicist P. A. M. Dirac (born 1902) said that the new physics "explains all of chemistry and most of physics." This is a bold claim, but probably a pretty accurate one.

This magnificent structure of knowledge was built by many men. A large number of them were trying to answer the simple question we asked at the start of Chapter 2: What is light?

By the middle of the twentieth century, that question had been answered well enough to lead scientists onto the path of the laser.

4
Men Who Made the Laser

Who invented the laser?

That depends on what you mean by "invented." In 1960, the American physicist Theodore Maiman built the first successful laser. At that time he was a member of the scientific staff of the Hughes Aircraft Company's Research Laboratories, in Malibu, California. Later he became head of the Korad Division of Union Carbide Corporation.

But Maiman was following predictions made by other scientists who had shown theoretically that it might be possible to make a laser. And these men were following the work of others. As we saw in the last chapter, we could even include Galileo and Newton on the list of those who helped invent the laser. That would be stretching things though. If we consider only those men whose work led *directly* to the laser, we can make a much shorter list.

EINSTEIN: STIMULATED EMISSION

As with almost everything that's happened in physics in this century, we would have to begin with Einstein.

In 1917, after publishing both his special and general theories of relativity and his work on the photoelectric effect, Einstein became interested in the way a gas will absorb and give off energy. This problem was somewhat in the same area that Planck was looking into when he first hit on the quantum theory.

Einstein found that there are three processes involved in the way a gas absorbs or gives off energy.

First there's *absorption*. This happens when a quantum of energy—a photon—comes into the gas and interacts with one of its atoms. The photon is absorbed by the atom, and the atom gains energy. As we saw in the previous chapter, the atom is said to be in an excited state.

Then there's *emission*. Emission takes place when the excited atom's electron hops down from its high-energy orbit to a lower orbit and gives off a photon in the process. This is actually called *spontaneous emission*, since the atom de-excites itself spontaneously, that is, with no outside forces acting upon it.

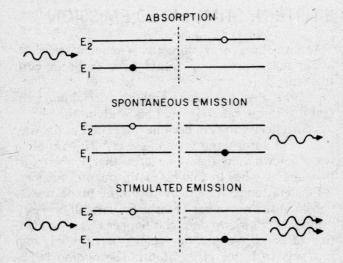

We saw both absorption and spontaneous emission when we examined Bohr's explanation of the energy states of the hydrogen atom. Einstein used Bohr's ideas to explain how energy gets into and out of a gas. But Einstein added one more important process.

He recognized that there are times when an atom might be in the excited state and is struck by a photon. In this case, Einstein predicted, the atom won't get more excited. Its electron will drop back to a lower orbit and give off a photon, just as in spontaneous emission. And the original photon that struck the atom won't be absorbed at all but will continue on its way. So we have two photons where there had been only one before.

Einstein called this phenomenon *stimulated emission*. It was an interesting curiosity, this business of getting two photons for one, but only a curiosity, in 1917. After all, stimulated emission hardly ever happens in the natural world. Excited atoms almost always drop back to their lowest-energy ground states in times like a few millionths of a second. They produce spontaneous emission, but the atoms don't stay in the excited state long enough to give stimulated emission a chance to take place.

So for nearly half a century, stimulated emission was considered to be interesting, but of no practical use. Today the words "stimulated emission" give us two letters in the acronym *laser*.

TOWNES: THE MASER

After the great leap forward that all of physics made in the first decades of the twentieth century, a leap that included quantum mechanics and relativity, things settled down once again. Men had gained important new insights into the workings of the physical world. Now was the time to polish this raw new knowledge, to test it and make certain that it was correct, to fill in the blank spaces that had been overlooked in the first rush of new ideas.

Slowly the new knowledge began to be applied by scientists and engineers to making new inventions, new "gadgets." One of them was the nuclear bomb. Another was the maser. And, finally, came the laser.

In 1950 no one in the world could guess that there would ever be such a thing as the laser. It wasn't predicted, it wasn't looked for—not in 1950.

Many scientists were searching hard for better ways to make radars though. And in 1951 this search led the American physicist Charles Townes to begin thinking about a device that ultimately became known as the *maser*. This was the forerunner of the laser, although no one knew it then.

Townes was a professor of physics at Columbia University in 1951. Earlier he had worked at Bell Telephone Research Laboratories, where much of the original research in communications and radar was performed during and after World War II. Bell Labs is still an important factor in communications research, and much work on lasers has been done there.

But we're getting ahead of our story.

Townes was interested in radar, not light. During World War II and afterward, he had done research on methods to make radars more precise. Much of his work, by 1950, dealt with the *microwave* region of the electromagnetic spectrum, where wavelengths are a few centimeters long. Microwaves are much shorter than ordinary radio and radar wavelengths and only slightly longer than infrared.

The heart of a radar transmitter is a metal box, or cavity, that's called the "resonator." The resonator works someting like the hollow sound box of a violin or guitar, where sound waves bounce back and forth and then emerge in the proper form to please us. In a radar's resonator, electromagnetic waves are "bounced," or made to oscillate.

You know that to make higher notes (which are shorter wavelengths) a stringed instrument must be made smaller. A violin is smaller than a bass fiddle.

The same principle holds true for electromagnetic wave resonators. To make radars of shorter wavelength the resonator must be made smaller. Of course, there's a practical limit to how small you can make an electromagnetic resonator.

Or is there? Townes hit on the idea of using atoms themselves as resonators. Actually, when the first experiments were done at Columbia, Townes's team used molecules of ammonia rather than individual atoms. The ammonia molecule contains one atom of nitrogen and three of hydrogen, linked together in a pyramid shape.

Meanwhile, as so often happens in science, another researcher was on the same trail. In 1952, Joseph Weber, then studying for his doctor's degree at Catholic University, in Washington, D.C., described exactly the same idea of using atoms or molecules as resonators to produce microwave radiation.

The idea was on its way. In Russia, at the Lebedev Institute of Physics, A. M. Prokhorov and N. G. Basov were also working in the same area. But it was Townes, at Columbia, who got there first. He worked with two graduate students, H. J. Zeiger and James P. Gordon, plus several other assistants.

They worked with ammonia gas, and with electromagnetic energy at a wavelength of 1.25 centimeters. This is a frequency of 24,000 megacycles per second. Since the unit called the *hertz* is equal to one cycle per second, we can use the term 24,000 "megahertz." A frequency of 24,000 megahertz means that the electromagnetic wave oscillates from crest to crest 24,000 million times each second.

When ammonia gas is irradiated with electromagnetic energy of 24,000-megahertz frequency, the ammonia molecules become excited. This particular frequency has the right quantum energy to excite the ammonia molecules into a high-energy state. Under normal conditions the molecules will quickly fall back to their ground state, undergoing spontaneous emission in the process. And, of course, they will emit photons of 24,000 megahertz. (1.25-centimeter wavelength) as they return to the ground state.

Under ordinary conditions, spontaneous emission takes place in some of the molecules while others are being excited. The situation is something like a normal day at a bank. Some customers are depositing money and others are withdrawing it. Some ammonia molecules are being excited while others are falling back to the ground state through spontaneous emission. This is an *equilibrium* condition.

Although there's a considerable amount of energy being transferred within the gas under equilibrium conditions, the energy is simply going from one molecule to another. It's too disorganized to be of much use.

But what if you could arrange things so that a large number of the molecules become excited together and emit photons together? Then the energy output would be highly organized—and useful. This is something like a "run" on the bank, when everybody wants to withdraw his money at the same time. Fortunately, things can be arranged so that fresh energy can be supplied to the gas, and the molecular bank won't run out of energy "money."

Townes and his co-workers tried to accomplish this. They used the 24,000-megahertz radiation to excite the ammonia molecules, then tried to keep them at the excited, high-energy state while more 24,000-megahertz energy was applied. Einstein predicted that this should produce stimulated emission. An avalanche of photons, all at the 1.25-centimeter wavelength, should stream from the ammonia molecules.

The big problem was to hold the molecules in the

excited state. Under ordinary equilibrium conditions the excited molecules quickly fall back to the ground state. This cannot be tolerated when you are seeking stimulated emission.

Happily, the ammonia molecule acts in a very helpful way when it is exposed to a strong electrical field. Excited ammonia molecules are repelled by a strong electrical field, whereas molecules in the lower-energy state are attracted by such fields. If you have an equilibrium gas, where some of the molecules are excited and some are not, you can pass the gas through an electric-field "separator" to get a stream of molecules that are almost entirely in the excited state.

This *nonequilibrium* gas of excited molecules can be stimulated by the proper energy quanta and give off a cascade of photons.

Simple in theory, it took Townes and his co-workers more than two years to make the device work. Late in 1953 their ammonia system "turned on." It produced a monotone signal at 24,000 megahertz, a pure song that rang sweetly for the happy scientists.

Nothing like this had ever been seen before. All other electronic oscillators produced a rather broad band of frequencies, no matter how carefully they were tuned. But this new device, this molecular oscillator, produced one frequency and one frequency only.

The device was so new that there wasn't even a name for it. Eventually the term *maser* was coined, standing for Microwave Amplification by Stimulated Emission of Radiation. In other words, microwave

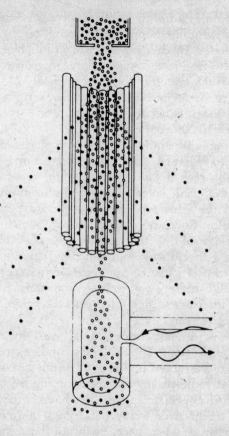

In the maser, electromagnetic energy excites the ammonia molecules (top). An electrial field separator (center) sorts out the excited (white) molecules, which are stimulated to give off a cascade of photons (bottom), producing an electromagnetic wave of one frequency only.

153

radiation is amplified—made stronger—through the use of stimulated emission of radiation.

Actually, Townes's maser wasn't much of an amplifier. It produced a very pure microwave output, but a weak one. Its "song" at precisely 24,000 megahertz made an excellent clock however. An ammonia maser clock is accurate to within one second over a span of 10,000 years!

Nicolaas Bloembergen, a Dutch physicist who had come to Harvard University, showed in 1956 that it was theoretically possible to build a maser out of solid materials such as iron and chromium. He predicted that this type of maser would make a good amplifier. Soon there were many laboratories trying to build a solid-state maser amplifier. Both Bell Telephone Laboratories and Lincoln Laboratory of the Massachusetts Institute of Technology were successful. The MIT maser was a true amplifier: a relatively weak microwave signal fed into the maser came out much stronger.

Masers quickly found many uses in radar and communications. They helped to make extremely sensitive radio receivers that can be tuned in on the very faintest radio-wave emissions coming from very distant star clusters. Thus masers have helped astronomers to discover many new types of radio signals coming from deep space. So far all these signals have apparently been completely natural in origin. But if we ever find radio messages from an intelligent race out among the stars, it will be the maser that has helped to make the discovery possible.

Incidentally, much of the research that led to the

maser was paid for by the U.S. Government. The Defense Department, in particular, has spent many, many millions of dollars to improve radar and radio systems. So some tongue-in-cheek scientists have said that the word "maser" could also be an acronym for Means of Acquiring Support for Expensive Research.

TOWNES AND SCHAWLOW: THE OPITICAL MASER

While masers were being developed to the point where they became useful tools for electronics engineers, Townes was busy with new ideas. The maser produced electromagnetic waves at wavelengths shorter than any other electronic device. Could still-shorter wavelengths be produced?

In the electromagnetic spectrum, next to the microwave region is the area of infrared waves, and then visible light.

Townes began working together with his brother-in-law, Arthur L. Schawlow, who was a research physicist at Bell Labs. They had collaborated years earlier on a book about microwaves. Now they began studying the possibilities of producing a maser that gave off light waves instead of microwaves. They spoke of it as an *optical maser*.

Today we call it the laser.

5
The Pulsing Ruby Shines

Townes and Schawlow knew what they needed to make an optical maser.

They had to find a type of molecule or atom that could be "pumped up" to an excited state and then kept there without undergoing spontaneous emission, so that a large number of excited atoms of molecules could be held in readiness. Then a few photons of the right wavelength would cause stimulated emission, and the entire population of excited atoms or molecules would give off a cascade of photons—all of the same wavelength—while falling back to the lower-energy level of the ground state.

This trick of getting atoms or molecules into the excited state and then holding them there is called *population inversion*. Under normal conditions, a group of atoms tends to stay at the lowest possible energy level, as we've seen. Excited atoms or molecules "want" to fall back quickly to the ground state. At any given moment, most of the atoms or molecules in a large group under equilibrium conditions are in the ground state, and very few are in the excited state.

Physicists say that the ground state is *well populated* and the excited state *poorly populated*. This is the equilibrium condition, the condition that normally prevails—unless something unusual happens.

It's something like the situation around a crowded swimming pool. Most of the people are either floating in the water or resting at poolside. Only a few are up on the high diving board at any one moment, and these few quickly dive back into the water.

To make a laser you need a population inversion, that is, the reverse of normal conditions. The atoms must be excited into a high-energy state and then held there for a while. The ground state is almost depopulated while the excited state gets crowded. It's as if almost everyone at the swimming pool climbed up to the high board at once and then teetered there waiting for something to happen.

What happens in a laser, of course, is that a few photons of the right wavelength can cause all the excited atoms to give off photons by stimulated emission. An avalanche, or cascade, of photons is produced.

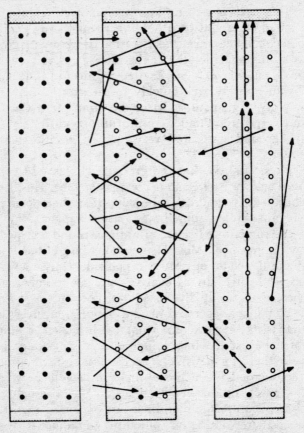

How a laser works: white circles are excited atoms; arrows indicate photons. As the photons are reflected back and forth, excited atoms give off more and more photons by stimulated emission until a cascade of photons is emitted in unified, coherent, single-direction waves

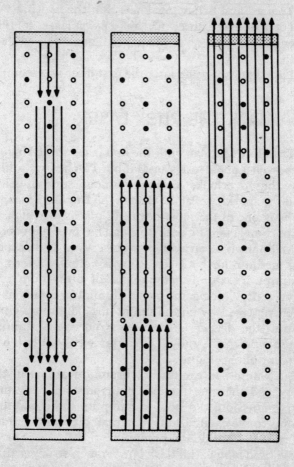

Townes and Schawlow knew that this is what was needed to make an optical maser—or laser. In 1958 they published a scientific paper that explained their ideas.

Less than two years later the first laser was shining.

MAIMAN: THE RUBY LASER

Theodore Maiman built the first laser at the Hughes Research Laboratories in Malibu. Perched on a hilltop that overlooks Malibu's famous surfing beach and the sparkling Pacific Ocean, the Hughes Research Labs is one of the most beautiful places at which an important scientific breakthrough has ever happened.

Maiman chose an artificial ruby crystal as the working medium for his laser. Ruby is actually a form of aluminum oxide, a compound of aluminum and oxygen, in which some of the aluminum atoms have been replaced by chromium atoms. The more chromium, the deeper is the ruby's red color. Maiman chose a pale-pink ruby that contained about half of 1 percent of chromium.

He wanted to excite the chromium atoms in the ruby and then get them to emit photons by stimulated emission. But how to pump up the chromium atoms to the excited state? Maiman hit upon the idea of making light do the pumping.

He used a powerful flash lamp, much stronger than the flash lamps we use with cameras for taking indoor photographs. Maiman knew that when ruby crystals are exposed to strong pulses of light, they *fluoresce.* That is, the chromium atoms in the ruby are excited by the burst of light energy, but they immediately drop back to the ground state by spontaneous emission. All that happens is that the ruby puts out a short burst of ordinary light, something like the pale glow of a fluorescent watch dial.

But Maiman thought that if the flash lamp's burst of light could be intense enough, it could trigger laser action. Instead of the pale glow of fluorescence, he would get a narrow beam of intensely powerful laser light.

Maiman's ruby was a tiny cylinder, only 4 centimeters long and ½ centimeter in diameter. The ends of this tiny rod were polished flat and partially silvered so that they became mirrors, but mirrors that would reflect light only up to a certain intensity. If and when the light got strong enough, these partially silvered mirrors would allow the light to go through them and leave the ruby altogether.

A helical flash lamp was placed around the ruby rod, coiling about it so that its light would strike the entire surface of the rod. When the lamp flashed, it broadcast a strong burst of light in all directions.Some of this light energy went into the ruby and excited the chromium atoms—the first step toward laser action.

The chromium atom can reach two excited energy levels under these conditions. Once it has reached either of these levels, it immediately falls back to an intermediate energy level—not the ground state, but an excited state that's about halfway between the ground level and the highest energy level it can reach.

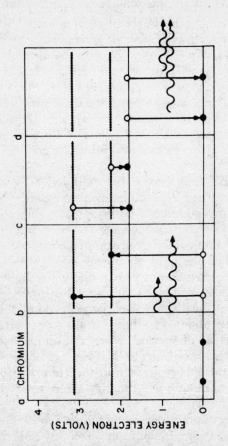

The chromium atoms are excited (b) to high energy levels, drop back (c) to a metastable state, and (d) drop to ground level, emitting photons of the same wavelength as incoming photons which start further reactions

The chromium atoms tend to stay at this intermediate level for a few thousandths of a second. This is
a long time in the frenetic world of atoms. At this
point, they are said to be in a *metastable state*.
*Meta*stable means partially stable; that is, when the
atoms stay at an excited energy level for as long as a
few milliseconds, they are considered to be in a partially stable condition, not as stable as being in the
ground state, of course, but much more stable than
the flicker of time that the atoms remain in the very
highest energy levels.

While they're in this metastable state, a few of the
chromium atoms spontaneously emit photons and
drop back to the ground level. These spontaneously
emitted photons are the first few pebbles that start
the landslide.

The photons strike other chromium atoms in their
excited, metastable state. And since the photons are
at exactly the right wavelength, they produce stimulated emission. Each time a photon strikes a metastable chromium atom, another photon of the same
wavelength is produced. Now the two photons go on
to strike two other metastable chromium atoms.

The photons are moving in all directions, moving
at random—up, down, left, right—but always in
straight lines. Many of them escape from the ruby
rod right away, but a number of them happen to be
moving in a direction that is along the axis of the
rod. They get as far as the mirrored end of the rod,
and then they are turned around, reflected back in
the direction from which they came.

So they go streaming down the length of the rod,

banging into more metastable atoms along the way and causing more stimulated emission, making a bigger and bigger cascade of photons. They strike the other mirrored end of the road and are reflected back again.

The cascade gets stronger and stronger each time the photons are bounced off the mirrored ends and reverse direction. But this happens only to the photons that are moving exactly along the axis of the rod. Photons that travel off axis quickly leave the ruby.

All this takes place in a few millionths of a second (microseconds). You can calculate for yourself how long it takes light, traveling at 300,000 kilometers per second, to travel the length of a 4-centimeterslong rod!

When the cascade of photons reaches a high-enough intensity, it passes through the partially silvered mirror at one end of the ruby and comes out as a pulse of brilliant laser light.

Maiman's original laser produced a pulse of light at 6,942 angstrom units, which was the wavelength he expected. (One angstrom equals 10^{-8} centimeter.) The pulse was about half a millisecond in duration.

WHAT MAKES LASER LIGHT SO DIFFERENT?

We took a glimpse at the differences between laser light and ordinary light in Chapter 1. We said earlier that lasers produce light that's brighter, more directional, monochromatic, and coherent. Now we can begin to understand why.

Intensity. Laser light is brighter than any other type of light source because we arrange things in the laser so that a very high percentage of the excited atoms contribute their photons to the light output. In ordinary light sources—for example, the flash lamp that pumps a ruby laser—only a few of the atoms are giving up photons at any one instant of time. In the laser, the atoms have been organized much better.

It's something like what happens when a crowd of people yell at a football game. If the people holler at random, individually, there's a steady hum of noise. But if the cheerleaders get them all to shout together, the sound can rock the stadium.

Directionality. Here again, we've arranged things to make the laser beam very narrow. This is a feature of the shape, or geometry, of the laser rod. The photons that come out as laser light, as we've seen, are those that have traveled back and forth along the axis of the ruby rod. Photons that move in other directions are lost. So the laser pulse comes out in a very narrow beam, which spreads very little and thus can carry an extremely long way. In this regard, lasers are somewhat like precision, long-range rifles, whereas other light sources are like shotguns.

A drawback, though, comes from those photons that travel off axis and so are lost. Just as much pumping energy was invested in them as in the photons that come out in the laser beam. Therefore each lost photon represents a lowering of the laser's efficiency. And most lasers are rather low in efficiency.

Monochromacity. By now you should understand why laser light is monochromatic. Only photons of the same wavelength can be emitted—well, almost. Actually, Maiman found that this earliest laser wasn't quite truly monochromatic. It emitted a narrow band of wavelengths clustered around the 6,943-angstrom line. The laser was much more truly monochromatic than any other light source, but its output wasn't exactly all at one single wavelength.

Different types of lasers vary in this regard, but, in general, lasers are the most monochromatic light sources yet discovered.

Coherence. Laser light is coherent, but light from other sources is not. In Chapter 1 we compared laser light to the precise march of West Point cadets, and light from other sources to the gyrations of an auditorium full of rock dancers.

If you could see light as a series of waves, then you would see that the waves coming out of a laser come out all in step, or in *phase*. They are all the same size, the same shape, and have the same spacing between them. The light waves are perpendicular to the direction in which they're moving; this is called *spatial coherence*. They are equally spaced, so that the time between one wave crest and the next is always the same; this is called *temporal coherence*.

THE FIRST GLOW OF ENTHUSIASM

With the first announcement of Maiman's successful laser, scientists, military men, news reporters, leaders of industry, and even the everyday man in the street became excited about the new invention.

Here was something straight from science fiction, but now it was real! Now we can have "energy beams" that will cut through metals, "radiation weapons" that will shoot down missiles, "bloodless scalpels" that will make extremely delicate incisions in a patient's flesh and cauterize (scar or burn) the blood vessels that are cut, closing them immediately and preventing bleeding.

Engineers soon began to show some of the tricks the laser could do: for example, a single pulse from a powerful ruby laser could blast a hole through a razor blade. This was only a demonstration, the engineers explained. Better things were on the way. Schawlow enjoyed showing people how a laser beam could go through a clear balloon without damaging it, but exploded a dark-colored balloon inside the transparent one.

Many companies, large and small, began to work on laser research and development. New companies sprang up to build lasers and sell them.

Gradually, the first rush of enthusiasm wore off. It became clear that lasers wouldn't solve everybody's problems. In fact, although lasers were exciting and wonderful, people began to doubt that there were *any* really useful jobs for them to do outside the laboratory. Lasers were expensive and really very inefficient. And even though they could deliver extremely intense bursts of light, their total power output was quite low.

By 1965, many scientists and engineers were saying that "the laser is a solution in search of a problem."

We'll see in the final chapters of this book that lasers have now found many, many problems that they can solve better, faster, and ultimately cheaper than any other device. But it took ten years of hard work to match the laser to these problems.

6
Solid, Gas, and Liquid Lasers

Maiman's pulsed ruby laser opened the floodgates. During the decade of the 1960's, physicists and engineers all over the world turned out many types of lasers, using many different substances as the "lasing" material. Laser action was produced in solids, gases, and liquids. Even the semiconductor materials used to make transistors were turned into lasers.

A high school boy in Boston's Roxbury ghetto built a homemade laser by using the glass tube from a burned-out fluorescent lamp, the compressor motor from an old refrigerator, and a lot of ingenuity. The material that "lased" was gaseous, a mixture of carbon dioxide, nitrogen, and water vapor, with some slight traces of other gases mixed in. Where did he get this gas mixture? From his own breath!

Ordinary air has been made to "lase" (actually, the nitrogen in the air produced laser action; the oxygen and other gases didn't). Laser light has also been coaxed from uranium crystals mixed with fluorides—but not exactly the type of fluoride mixture that's used in toothpaste!

In general, lasers can be classified by either the material that's used to produce laser action or the method of exciting the active atoms or molecules. This excitation method is often called "pumping."

There are many types of solid-state lasers that use crystalline material such as ruby or glass. The most common are the rubies, synthetic garnets called YAG (after the materials yttrium, aluminum, and garnet), and glass that contains atoms of the yellowish metal neodymium. These crystal and glass lasers are optically pumped, usually with flash lamps similar to the one first used by Maiman.

Liquid lasers too are generally optically pumped. Gas lasers are excited electrically, and so are the semiconductor lasers. Then there are chemical lasers, where the laser excitation comes from mixing together two or more very energetic materials such as fluorine and hydrogen to get a strong chemical reaction that pumps up the laser atoms or molecules.

LASER ENERGY AND POWER

Before we look at these other types of lasers, we should spend a moment on the energy and power output of lasers. Since we're going to be talking about energy and power, we'll need to know what the terms *joule* and *watt* mean.

The joule is a unit of energy, and energy is a measure of the ability to do work. For example, it takes a certain amount of work to heat up a cup of coffee. The energy needed to raise the temperature of a cup of coffee by 10 degrees centigrade is slightly more than 5,000 joules. So you can see that the joule is really a rather tiny amount of energy.

Power is energy divided by time. If an energy of 1 joule is produced for a period of 1 second, we can say that a power of 1 watt has been produced. Like the joule, the watt is a small unit. It takes 746 watts to equal 1 horsepower. How many watts can your family automobile's engine deliver?

For pulsed lasers, such as the earliest rubies, we can express output in terms of the power produced by each pulse or the energy in each pulse. Ruby lasers can now routinely deliver up to a billion watts (10^9 watts or a gigawatt) per pulse. But the pulse duration is very short, only a fraction of a second. If the laser's pulse duration is 5 microseconds (5×10^{-6} sec), then a pulse of 10^9 watts amounts to only 200 joules of energy—just about enough energy to heat our cup of coffee 1 degree centigrade!

171

But this seemingly small amount of energy can do fantastic things, mainly because it can be focused down to extremely high intensity. A laser beam can be focused down to a tiny spot, where the energy intensity is more than 10 million kilowatts (10^{10} watts) per square centimeter. By contrast, the most intense energy flux that sunlight can produce is 7 kilowatts per square centimeter, as we saw in Chapter 1.

JAVAN: THE GAS LASER

In 1959, not long after Townes and Schawlow's original paper on the optical maser, the Iranian-born physicist Ali Javan showed that it should be possible to produce laser action in a gas mixture. Javan was then on the staff of Bell Labs; he is now a professor at the Massachusetts Institute of Technology.

By 1961, Javan and a team of co-workers had produced the world's first gas laser.

Javan's laser used a mixture of helium and neon gases. These are *inert* gases; they don't engage in chemical reactions. Often they are called *noble gases* because they hold themselves chemically aloof from all the other elements, under normal circumstances. There are six noble gas elements: helium is the lightest, then comes neon, argon, krypton, xenon, and the radioactive radon.

In the helium-neon laser, the pumping energy is supplied directly by electricity. This is much more efficient than using electricity to make a flash lamp work and then using some of the flash lamp's photons to pump up the laser atoms. Javan's original helium-neon laser needed only 50 watts of electrical power to drive it, whereas ruby lasers need kilowatts of input power, or more.

The electrical energy gets into the laser gas through electrodes that cause a continuous spark, or *discharge*, through the gas. This is very much like what happens in an ordinary fluorescent lamp. The gas is sealed inside a long, thin glass tube, and the electrodes at either end of the tube produce an electrical discharge.

In Javan's laser, the electrons being pumped into the gas by the discharge collide mostly with the helium atoms, since the gas mixture is usually ten parts helium to one part neon. This excites the helium atoms to a high-energy level. Then the helium atoms collide with the neon atoms and transfer their energy by collision. Somewhat the same thing happens on a pool table. You hit the cue ball and give it enough energy to roll across the table. When the cue ball strikes another ball, some of the enrgy is transferred to the colored ball and it begins to roll. A really good pool shot can often transfer just about all the cue ball's energy to the colored ball, and the cue ball will stop dead after its collision.

So we have a situation where electrons excite the helium atoms, and the helium atoms collide with the neon atoms and excite them.

The neon atom can have several different excitation levels. Each of these different energy states produces a different-wavelength photon when the neon atom falls back toward the ground state. In Javan's original helium-neon laser, the output was at 11,500 angstroms, which is in the invisible infrared part of the spectrum.

Since then, the other possible wavelengths have been produced by operating the helium-neon laser under slightly different conditions. Today you can buy a helium-neon laser for about a hundred dollars. Many schools have done so and use the brilliant-red 6,328-angstrom beam to demonstrate many of the characteristics of light.

Like the ruby laser, the helium-neon laser uses two mirrors and depends on a cascade of photons to produce its beam of light. But unlike the original ruby laser, the helium-neon laser runs continuously; it will produce laser light as long as the electrical current is flowing in it. In laser engineering jargon, this is called *CW operation*. CW simply means "continuous wave," as opposed to pulsed operation. Helium-neon lasers are low-powered devices, usually producing about 50 milliwatts (0.05 watt).

OTHER GAS LASERS

Many other types of gas lasers have been developed since 1961. Among the most useful of these are the so-called *ion lasers*.

An ion is simply an atom that has lost one or more of its orbital electrons. When an atom loses an electron, it is left with more positive charges than negative. Then it is said to be an ion, with the understanding that it is a positively charged ion. (It is possible for an atom to gain an electron, which would give it an excess negative charge. In that case it is called a negative ion. Since negative ions are rare, when the term "ion" is used alone, it is understood to mean a positive ion.)

The argon ion laser has proved itself to be a versatile and popular device. As the name suggests, it operates on argon gas, which becomes ionized when an electrical discharge is applied to it. The argon atoms lose electrons, resulting in a gas mixture that has argon ions, free electrons, and some un-ionized argon atoms in it. An ionized gas is often called a *plasma* by physicists, and plasma is thought of as a fourth state of matter, since plasmas have properties different from those of gases, solids, or liquids.

The argon ion laser operates at any of ten different wavelengths, which can be selected at will. They range from the green 5,145 angstroms to 3,511 angstroms, which is in the invisible ultraviolet region. Power output of about 10 watts is common with argon ion lasers, and they can be operated either CW or pulsed.

Gas lasers have also been made from the vapors of heated metals, such as cadmium, tin, and zinc. At Bell Telephone Laboratories, small pellets of cadmium, tin, or zinc are placed in a laser tube, together with helium gas. A strong electrical current vaporizes the metal and produces laser action. Cadmium vapor produces either blue or ultraviolet light, depending on how the laser is run. Tin makes red light, and zinc gives infrared.

Copper vapor has also been used in lasers. As you

might guess from looking at copper objects that have been exposed to the air for some time, a copper vapor laser gives a brilliant green light.

The highest power produced to date by any type of laser has come from carbon dixide gas lasers. We'll look at them in some detail in the next chapter.

SEMICONDUCTOR LASERS

Most lasers are very inefficient. Generally they have efficiencies of only a few percent at most. The amount of power in the light beam is usually only a few percent of the electrical power that originally supplied either to drive the flash lamps in the case of crystal or glass lasers or to excite the gas in gas lasers.

In 1962, though, three separate research teams announced the invention of the *semiconductor laser*. This type of laser is also known as the *injection laser* or the *junction diode laser*.

The research teams worked separately, and each hit upon the semiconductor laser without knowing of the others' work. The teams were from the IBM Corporation, led by Marshall I. Nathan; MIT's Lincoln Laboratory, headed by Robert H. Rediker; and General Electric Company's Research Laboratory in Schenectady, under Robert N. Hall.

Semiconductor lasers have some intriguing advantages over other types. First, they are relatively efficient, better than 10 percent. They are excited electrically and operate in pulses—extremely rapid pulse rates, too, since 5,000 to 10,000 pulses per second are commonplace. Their output is mainly in the infrared region of the spectrum, from 8,500 to 9,100 angstroms. However, certain types of semiconductor lasers can get up into the red end of the visible specturm as far as 6,100 angstroms, and others have gone farther into the infrared, down to wavelengths of about 3 microns or 30,000 angstroms.

Semiconductor lasers are *small*. The first few ever made were only a millimeter or so long. They resemble the transistors in your miniature radio. Naturally, their power output is also small. Peak pulse power of 60 watts is about the best you can buy on the commercial market, although *arrays* of several such lasers bundled together have been designed to give up to a kilowatt or so per pulse.

The semiconductor laser resembles the transistor in many ways. They are both made of semiconducting materials, that is, materials that have a variable degree of electrical conductivity: elements such as germanium, arsenic, and phosphorus.

In the semiconductor laser, electrons do all the work. A typical semiconductor laser is made of gallium arsenide phosphide. Small but carefully controlled amounts of impurities in this exotic mixture of elements produce a tiny semiconductor that has mostly positive electrical charges on one side of it and mostly negative electrical charges on the other side. The junction between these two regions is where laser action takes place.

When an electrical current is applied to the semiconductor, it forces electrons to move from the negative region to the positive region. The electrons are excited when they move, and as they pass the junction between the two regions, they emit photons. The two ends of the tiny semiconductor are flattened and highly polished so that they act as mirrors and build up a photon cascade.

By controlling the temperature of the semiconductor and the frequency of the incoming electrical current, the wavelength of the laser's output can be changed over a considerable span. Most gallium arsenide phosphide lasers, for example, can be made to emit at any wavelength between 8,500 and 9,100 angstroms.

A laser tiny enough to balance on your fingertip, with good efficiency and needing only a few watts of electricity to drive it! A laser that emits in the infrared at thousands of pulses per second! Semiconductor lasers are finding many uses in short-range communications and radar systems, and in interesting jobs such as burglar alarms.

LIQUID LASERS

Early in 1963 a team of researchers at General Telephone and Electronics' Research Laboratories, headed by Alexander Lempicki and H. Samuelson, produced the first liquid laser.

Liquid lasers employ highly complex molecules. The first liquid lasers produced laser light from atoms of europium, a rare-earth element. The europium atoms were linked to a complex type of molecule called a *chelate*. Most of these complex molecules are made up in large part of long chains of carbon atoms. They are called *organic molecules* since they are of the type found in living creatures.

Although the chemical composition of liquid lasers is complex, in many ways their operation is similar to that of crystal lasers such as the ruby. The goal is to get laser action from the desired atoms—europium, in the earliest liquid lasers. The rest of the liquid material is there to help excite the europium and hold it in the excited state long enough for stimulated emission to begin.

By 1970, several different types of organic molecules had been made to lase. And it was found that some of these liquids—now generally called "dyes"—can be tuned to produce many different laser wavelengths. There are several different types of tunable dye lasers, and they're pumped either by flash lamps or by another laser. Some of these turnable dye lasers can give you any wavelength you desire across the entire visible part of the spectrum.

CHEMICAL LASERS

As we have said earlier, a laser needs an outside source of energy to pump its atoms or molecules to a high-energy excited state. This energy is usually electricity, either for a flash lamp or for direct excitation. Most lasers are inefficient and waste most of the electricity used on them.

In chemical lasers the situation is very different.

The chemicals that produce laser action also provide the pumping energy. There's no need for an outside energy source. Chemical lasers offer the promise of being much simpler and much more efficient than other types of lasers.

Their major drawback is that they require chemicals such as fluorine, chlorine, hydrogen, and others that are tricky to handle and can be dangerous. And once a batch of these chemicals has been used to produce laser light, it can't easily be reused again. The chemical laser must be constantly supplied with fresh chemicals.

The first chemical laser was produced in 1964 by Jerome V. V. Kasper and George C. Pimentel at the University of California at Berkeley. Several other types of chemical lasers have operated successfully since then.

In general, chemical lasers require the type of chemical reaction that is called *exothermic*, that is, chemical reactions that release heat. (Chemical reactions that absorb heat are called *endothermic*.)

One of the first chemical lasers used hydrogen and chlorine as its working elements. It wasn't a "pure" chemical laser, however, because it needed a flash of ultraviolet light to get the reactions started.

Both the chlorine and the hydrogen start off in this case as two-atom molecules: Cl_2 and H_2. The UV flash lamp energy *dissociates* (breaks up) the chlorine molecule into separate atoms of chlorine. An atom of chlorine reacts with a molecule of H_2 to produce a hydrogen chloride molecule (HCl) and a free hydrogen atom.

All of this is the prelude. Now the free atom of hydrogen reacts with a chlorine molecule to produce another HCl molecule and a solitary chlorine atom, plus heat, since this is an exothermic reaction. But the HCl molecule produced in this reaction is in an excited, high-energy state. When struck by a photon of the proper wavelength, it undergoes stimulated emission. A few of the excited HCl molecules give off photons through ordinary spontaneous emission, and that's enough to start a cascade of stimulated emission from the rest of the excited HCl molecules.

Although the first chemical lasers needed UV energy to get them started, the pumping energy and laser action still came about as a result of chemical reactions. The UV flash was only a trigger to get things going. The chemical laser produced much more light energy output than the flash lamp put into the gas.

Research teams at Cornell University, Aerospace Corporation, and Avco Everett Research Laboratory have all announced successful chemical lasers. In general, such lasers produce output in the near-infrared region: from about 1- to 5-microns wavelengths.

The chemical laser offers the possibility of someday producing very high power at very good efficiency. But there's another type of gas laser that has already produced high power and good efficiency. It's time now to look at the carbon dioxide laser, which is beginning to resemble the heat ray of H. G. Wells's Martians.

7
High-Power Lasers

More than any other laser, the carbon dioxide laser is making the dreams of scientists and science fiction writers alike come true—and their nightmares too.

In many ways, the carbon dioxide laser is in a class by itself. Several different versions of it exist. One type has produced a continuous output of more than 400 kilowatts. Other types of carbon dioxide lasers have operated at efficiencies of better than 20 percent.

A gas laser, the carbon dioxide system is also called a *molecular laser,* since its laser energy comes from the carbon dioxide molecule (CO_2). Most of the chemical lasers now being developed are also molecular lasers.

C. K. N. Patel, of the Bell Telephone Laboratories, built the first carbon dioxide laser in 1965. At first glance, his CO_2 laser looked much like any gas laser. But studies had predicted that molecular lasers should be able to deliver very high power. And before long, beams of infrared radiation at 10.6-micron wavelengths were blasting through steel, burning through rock samples, and showering sparks all over the laser world.

THE NEED FOR NITROGEN . . .

Although CO_2 lasers depend on carbon dioxide for their powerful infrared output, they work best when the CO_2 is mixed with nitrogen.

What happens is this: the two-atom nitrogen molecule, N_2, is more easily excited by electrical energy than the three-atom CO_2 molecule. Luckily, the N_2 and CO_2 molecules tend to vibrate at almost exactly the same frequency, under the proper conditions. This means that we can excite the nitrogen molecules with an electrical current passed through the gas, and almost immediately the nitrogen will transfer most of the energy it has gained to the carbon dioxide molecules.

The CO_2 molecules are excited into the high-energy state by collisions with their N_2 neighbors. When a few of them emit photons due to spontaneous emission, a cascade of stimulated emission starts, all at the

10.6-micron wavelength. This process will continue as long as the electrical current goes through the gas mixture; the carbon dioxide laser is a CW device.

. . . AND SOMETHING EXTRA

Patel and other researchers quickly found out that the nitrogen-carbon dioxide laser works even better if still another gas is added to the mixture. Helium, oxygen, water vapor, and hydrogen have all been shown to be helpful.

The reason for this is that when a CO_2 molecule emits a photon at 10.6 microns, it doesn't fall all the way back to the ground state. It goes from a high-energy level to an intermediate level, where it remains for some time (a tiny fraction of a second, to be sure, but a long time in the molecular scale of things). The molecule can't be pumped up again by its nitrogen neighbors until it's brought back to the ground state. The third gas is put into the laser to deexcite the CO_2 molecule, return it to the ground state, so that it can be used once again to produce another laser action.

THE LONGER THE BETTER(?)

News travels fast in the scientific community, and the news of efficient, high-power molecular lasers spread almost with the speed of light itself. Carbon dioxide lasers were built in just about every laser lab in the world, and they proved to be capable of higher power and better efficiency than any previous laser.

Of course, the biggest ruby and neodymium-glass lasers had produced gigawatts of pulsed power for years. But they could only get off a few pulses per minute. Although their pulse energy was high, their average power was only 100 watts or so. The CO_2 laser soon began producing thousands of watts continuously.

Even before Patel's first successful CO_2 laser, several physicists had pointed out that gas lasers should be able to produce much higher power outputs than solids such as rubies. This is because gases are a higher-energy state of matter. The atoms or molecules of a gas have more energy invested in them than the atoms or molecules of a solid. To turn water into steam, you add energy. To turn water into ice, you take energy away.

But there seemed to be a curious problem in getting high power out of carbon dioxide lasers.

At first glance it would seem obvious that if a laser of a certain size produced, say, 500 watts, to get 1,000 watts you merely double the laser's size. Fine. How will you double the size? By making the laser tube twice as long or twice as fat?

Both ways were tried. Increasing the length of the CO_2 laser worked well enough. The laser output increased steadily as the length of the laser tube was made greater.

But increasing the diameter of the tube didn't increase the power output at all. Why should this be?

The answer is *heat*. As the laser operates, it produces heat; the electrical energy that doesn't come out of the laser as light comes out as waste heat. If the gas temperature gets too high, the laser will not work so well. The way to get rid of unwanted heat, in a long glass tube, is to let the heat escape through the walls of the tube.

Now, when you double the diameter of the tube, it contains more gas, but it's harder for most of this gas to get rid of its waste heat. There's a longer distance from the center of the tube to the outside walls. So fatter CO_2 lasers didn't produce more power because they couldn't get rid of the unwanted heat they produced.

But by keeping the laser tube thin and increasing its length, you could get more power. All the gas is still comfortably close to the cooling walls, and the waste heat gets out of the laser just as well as in a small tube.

So very long CO_2 lasers were built. One of them was built by the Army at Redstone Arsenal, Alabama. It was 53.4 meters long (178 feet) and produced nearly 3 kilowatts. Its intense, invisible beam could snap a steel knife blade almost instantly. The Army scientists and engineers who worked with it called it "Long Tom." They were careful to make certain that its business end didn't point toward the side of the building where they parked their cars!

BREAKTHROUGH: THE GAS DYNAMIC LASER

Although you could make a CO_2 laser more powerful by making it longer, there were practical limits on how long a laser you could build.

The Raytheon Company in 1968 built a carbon dioxide laser with a total length of 183 meters (600 feet). The laser tube was divided into fifteen segments of a little more than 12 meters each. The laser beam was bounced from one tube segment to another by mirrors, so that to the photons, it looked like one long continuous tube. This laser produced 8.8 kilowatts, the highest output then known.

But such cumbersome devices weren't very practical for much besides laboratory studies. A fragile glass tube of nearly 200 meters in length just isn't the kind of thing you would want in a factory, or on a battlefield. And it was difficult to transport the device and set all the tubes and mirrors in their correct alignment.

To make very high power lasers practical, some means of shrinking their size and making them more rugged had to be found.

It was.

In April, 1970, at the Washington meeting of the American Physical Society, Edward T. Gerry, of Avco Everett Research Laboratory, announced the *gas dynamic laser*.

The gas dynamic laser—or GDL, as it is often referred to—is based on a simple principle: flow the gas through the laser.

We have seen that one limitation on the power you can get out of a laser is the necessity to get rid of the waste heat that the laser generates. In solid lasers, such as the rubies, the heat must trickle through the crystal material of the laser rod and then escape from the rod's outer surface. In gas lasers, it works the same way, except that heat can flow through a gas more quickly. Still, for the heat to escape, it must make its way from the interior of the laser tube to the outside walls.

The gas dynamic idea is to move the gas, move it rapidly out of the laser as soon as it has yielded its laser energy. In a gas dynamic laser, the gas comes into the laser area through something like a wind tunnel. As the gas races through the laser section, it lases and then flows out, taking its waste heat with it, and is replaced by fresh gas that is ready for more laser action.

The gas dynamic laser that Gerry described is a carbon dioxide laser, and like all CO_2 lasers it emits at 10.6 microns.

But the GDL is *thermally pumped*, something different from all other lasers. A burner is used to produce a hot mixture of nitrogen, carbon dioxide, and water vapor. The hot gases flow through a tiny wind tunnel with nozzles scarcely a millimeter wide. When the gas comes out of these nozzles, it expands rapidly and cools down—with one vital exception.

Much of the energy that went into the gas in the burner, the thermal (heat) energy that made the gas hot, gets transferred at this point to the CO_2 molecules. They are excited into a high-energy state. Although the technique for exciting them is very different from Patel's original CO_2 laser, the molecules behave the same way.

As this excited gas mixture flows at supersonic speed through the miniature wind tunnel, it passes a set of mirrors. Stray photons build up a cascade of stimulated emission, and a powerful beam of 10.6-micron radiation emerges. The "used up" gas flows out of the laser area, and new gas comes in. The laser operates continuously, as long as the burner runs.

The first gas dynamic laser to use a burner produced power outputs of almost 10 kilowatts, not from a 200-meter-long glass tube, but from a metal laser section that was only slighter larger than a shoe box!

A larger GDL, described by Gerry as Avco's Mark V gas dynamic laser, has produced up to 60 kilowatts of continuous power. In a few minutes of operation, this one laser has turned out more power than all the other lasers in the world combined!

ADDING ELECTRICITY TO GAS DYNAMICS

The gas dynamic laser was indeed a breakthrough. But its efficiency was only a few percent. Electrically pumped CO_2 lasers had shown much better efficiencies, around 20 percent and even higher.

The obvious next step was to "marry" the gas dynamics idea with electrical pumping. Several research teams are now working on high-power, high-efficiency, electrically pumped, molecular gas lasers in which the gas is made to flow at high speeds. A. J. De Maria, of United Aircraft Research Laboratories, for example, has reported getting up to 11.5 kilowatts per meter of laser section in an electrically excited, flowing gas CO_2 laser.

Electrical GDL's can be made "closed cycle"; that is, the gas mixture can be routed back into the laser area after its waste heat has been removed. Thus the laser wouldn't need a continuous fresh supply of gas; it could use the same gas supply over and over again.

8
Frozen Light Rays

H. G. Wells foresaw lasers as weapons, and Buck Rogers, of the comic strips, had disintegrator rays that could melt steel in an eye blink. But no science fiction writer predicted the *hologram* and the three-dimensional pictures that lasers can produce.

Unlike the "zapping" of a metal target, with sparks flying in every direction, *holography* is a quiet and undramatic process that is about as exciting as taking a photograph—quiet, undramatic, and revolutionary.

For holography—making three-dimensional pictures by laser light—is already beginning to shatter many older ways of storing, handling, and moving information.

And information is the key to civilization. In a sense, our society depends on the information it can gather and use. Today you have access to far more information on just about any subject than all the emperors of Rome ever had. And our complex society depends on the sure, steady, speedy flow of information. When you find your favorite pickles on a supermarket shelf, it is because a network of information has gone from the farmlands, through the processing plants, transportation systems, warehouses, and the store itself to put that jar where you can get it.

Electrical power stations need to know how many kilowatts they will have to produce at each hour of the day. You want to know what tomorrow's weather is going to be. Information is the key to the way we live.

Lasers are starting to play several roles in the development of better, faster, more reliable information systems. One of the most fascinating parts of this development stems from the laser's ability to produce holographic pictures.

GABOR: THE HOLOGRAPH

In 1947, Dennis Gabor, of the Imperial College of Science and Technology, London, hit upon the idea for holography. This was thirteen years before the invention of the laser.

But Garbor wasn't interested in holography with light. He was working in the area of electron microscopes, and he wanted a way to make better electron "pictures" by using electron waves or X-rays. As often happens in life, his work never bore much fruit in the field in which he was interested. But it flowered in optical picture-making once the laser came along.

The idea behind holography is very simple, although quite different from ordinary photography. To make a photograph, you need a subject, a light source, photographic film of some sort, and an optical system. Light from the light source is reflected by the subject. The optical system focuses some of this reflected light onto the film and the film records the information through chemical changes in the film that are caused by the light—this is called a *photochemical* reaction.

In most cameras, the optical system is a glass lens or a series of lenses. But you can make your own simple camera by using nothing more than a pinhole as the optical system. All you need is a small box that can be tightly closed, so that no stray light can leak into it, and some means of keeping the film covered until you want to expose it. The light from the pinhole will cause a photochemical change just as surely as light that comes through the most elaborate set of lenses you can buy. But the pinhole will focus a clear, sharp image on the film only at one fixed distance, whereas lenses can be moved to focus over a wide range of distances.

Notice what happens when we make a photograph. The light waves that are reflected by the subject carry information about the subject's size, shape, color. When the light strikes the film, it makes an image of all this information in the chemicals of the film itself. And although the subject is three-dimensional, the film image has only two dimensions. We get something like a flat wall map of the round Earth.

The idea in holography is not to record an image of the subject, but to record the light waves that the subject has reflected. Instead of keeping an image on film, we keep the light waves themselves!

A hologram "freezes" the light waves we are interested in, so that we can "play back" their pattern later and see the subject that we originally started with. This is rather like recording a singer's voice so that you can hear it again whenever you want to.

Instead of a piece of film with an image on it, we have a hologram with a pattern of light waves. The hologram shows no image, no picture at all, only a confused swirl of interference patterns, the frozen record of light waves that were reflected by the subject. But the hologram has all the information we need to *reconstruct* the subject, to make the subject reappear in three dimensions, as solid and real looking as if it were actually standing in front of us.

ALONG COMES THE LASER

Holography was an interesting idea, but it wouldn't work unless you had a light source that was coherent. There was some hope of producing electron streams with the waves' fronts all lined up precisely, and Gabor and others worked in that area with X-rays for many years before 1960. As for visible light, everyone knew there were no practical sources of coherent light—until 1960. It wasn't long after the invention of the laser that Emmet N. Leith and Juris Upatnieks, of the University of Michigan, produced the first holographs.

They succeeded where others had failed mainly because they discovered that it wasn't enough merely to illuminate the subject with laser light. There had to be two patterns of light falling on the hologram: light reflected by the subject and unreflected light straight from the laser itself.

The two beams set up interference patterns—much like the patterns we created in our two-pinhole experiment in Chapter 2. These interference patterns are what the hologram records.

The light from the laser, then, shines partly on the subject and partly on a mirror. The subject reflects light in all directions; some of this reflected light falls on the hologram film, which is nothing more than ordinary photographic film, or an ordinary photographic plate in which the chemicals of the film are sandwiched between two sheets of glass.

Light waves from every part of the subject hit every part of the hologram film. And the undisturbed light straight from the laser bounces off the mirror and also hits the hologram film. This beam of light, which hasn't touched the subject at all, is called the *reference beam*.

The reflected light waves from the subject and

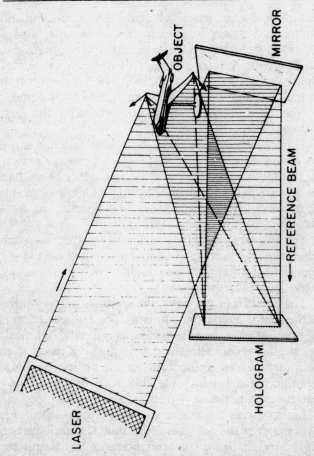

The laser beam reflected by an object interferes with the reference beam, creating a pattern of light called a hologram that can be recorded and used to reconstruct a three-dimensional picture of the object

196

from the reference beam set up patterns of bright reinforcement regions and dark cancellation regions as they interfere with each other. So we have a holograph, a recording of light waves. How do we play it back?

By shining the laser's beam on it. The original subject appears to take form in midair, as the laser shines through the film. The subject seems solid, three-dimensional. If we move around its image, we'll see it shift and reveal parts that were hidden from our view at first. We can even photograph the image if we want to. This "playback" process is called *reconstruction*.

Actually, holographic images don't look quite as real as the original subjects, partly because the holographic images have a slight twinkling in them. This is due to some of the microscopic interactions between laser light and the air it travels through; a researcher may find a way of overcoming it someday. Recently, research teams have discovered ways of reconstructing holograms with ordinary white light. And holographic pictures in color, even moving pictures, have been made.

There is an extremely interesting twist to holography. Remember that we said that light waves from every part of the subject fall on every part of the hologram? This means that the tiniest scrap of the hologram *contains all the information* that the entire hologram does.

You can tear off a piece of hologram and still get a complete, three-dimensional picture out of it. The image formed from the scrap may be blurry and blotchy, but all the information will be there. Thus holograms can be made very small and still carry a tremendous amount of information.

LASERS AND COMPUTERS

Lasers and holograms are starting a major revolution in the size, capacity, speed, and usefulness of computers.

First, consider a computer's memory. A good-sized computer of 1970 could store some 100 million "bits" of information in a few consoles that are about the size of a large kitchen refrigerator.

A hologram is an information-storage tool. A single hologram that is only 1 centimeter square (about the size of one side of a sugar cube) could store as many data bits as 4,000 cubic centimeters of standard computer memory core. Four thousand cubic centimeters is equal to slightly more than 14 cubic feet. If you have a 14-cubic-foot refrigerator in your kitchen, imagine squeezing down all the data bits it can hold to the size of one side of a sugar cube!

Holographic memories, then, will allow computer engineers to build machines that are fantastically smaller than modern computers. And by using laser beams for getting the information out of the memory and displaying it on a screen something like your TV screen, the computer will be able to work faster than any computer now running.

It's surprising to know that the basic idea for computers is about 150 years old. In 1822 the English mathematician Charles Babbage tried to build a mechanical computer. In theory, Babbage's machine was very much like the electronic computers of today. But Babbage didn't have electricity, let alone electronics. His machine used mechanical gears and steam power. It never worked right. It was too big, too clumsy, too slow. Babbage died an embittered man. His biographer claims that he used to fly into a rage whenever he saw an organ grinder and his monkey.

With the advent of vacuum tubes and electronic engineering, more than a century later, the first electronic computers were built. But they were so big that they needed whole floors of large buildings. And the heat that their tubes generated required minor Niagaras of cooling water.

By 1960 transistors had replaced the vacuum tubes, and printed circuits had taken the place of the miles of wires inside computers. They now became small enough, fast enough, and smart enough to help men reach the Moon, to guide entire automated factories, and even to keep the family checking account straight.

With lasers and holograms, computers could become truly drawer-sized. And cheap enough for almost anyone to buy.

Many people fear computers. Some fear the thought of a machine that will outsmart man. Others fear the uses that computers can be put to: when department stores, the Government, your employer and insurance company and bank, all have computer files about you, there's very little privacy left to your life. This can be a real threat to freedom.

But in a larger sense, computers can do for men's

brains exactly what machinery has done for our muscles. No man would dream of digging the foundations for a building by hand, not when there are power tools available. They work faster and cheaper than men do. Computers can help in the same way. Any job that can be done in the same way, over and over again, computers can do. Computers can free men for the truly creative jobs, the tasks that require new ideas, original thinking. Why should a man spend most of his life on an assembly line, doing the same dull chore over and over again, when a computer-directed tool can do the same thing?

When computers are cheap enough to be everywhere, men could enter a new era of freedom from drudgery. Lasers and holographs can help speed that day.

LASERS IN COMMUNICATIONS

In theory, a single laser beam could carry some 10 million television broadcasts at once!

Of course, it will be some time before laser communications beams are anywhere near that good. But, already, television and voice transmissions have been sent over distances of many kilometers by laser.

Like ordinary radio and television transmitters, lasers put out waves of electromagnetic energy. But light waves are much shorter and higher in frequency than the waves used now for radio and television. Commercial television broadcasts use wavelengths of 1 to 10 centimeters, which is equivalent to frequencies of between 50 and 500 megahertz. Light waves, which are on the order of 10^{-4} centimeter in wavelength and 10,000 gigahertz (10^{13} cycles per second) can carry enormously more information. It is similar to the difference between the printing on an outdoor advertising sign and the printing on the head of a pin.

The higher the frequency of the electromagnetic waves, the more waves you have available each second for using as message carriers. Since light waves vibrate at frequencies of about 100,000 to a million times faster than radio and television waves, they can carry that much more information. In the jargon of the electronics engineer, this information-carrying capacity is referred to as *bandwidth*. Visible light has a much broader bandwidth than radio waves.

The idea of communicating by light is hardly new. Ancient peoples used mirrors to reflect sunlight and signal one another across the valleys and open plains. Ships have used signal lamps with shutters on them to flick out Morse-code light flashes. And Alexander Graham Bell (1847–1922), inventor of the telephone, also invented a *photophone* in 1880. The photophone carried sounds on a ray of sunlight that was reflected off a vibrating mirror.

Electronic communications such as radio waves have two tremendous advantages over earlier methods of sending signals. First, radio waves can be *modulated*—coded—in such a way that they can carry very complex signals, including voices and even television pictures. Second, radio waves can travel for long distances. Some frequencies bounce off reflecting layers high in the atmosphere and "skip" across whole continents and oceans. The VHF and UHF signals used for television broadcasts are not reflected by these atmospheric layers, however, and television broadcasts carry only as far as the horizon, unless the signal is carried through cables or relayed by tall antennas or satellites.

As you know, radio waves can be modulated in two ways: amplitude modulation (AM) or frequency modulation (FM). In amplitude modulation, the height of the waves is altered, and this carries the "code" of information. In frequency modulation, the actual frequency of the waves is altered, with the waves bunched up at one point and spaced out at another, to carry the desired information.

Laser beams can be either amplitude or frequency modulated by several different means. Both techniques have been shown to work.

Lasers have great advantages as communications beams, but also some problems.

One of the greatest advantages, of course, is the laser's stupendous bandwidth. A thousand telephone signals, each with an individual bandwidth of 3,800 cycles per second, could be handled by a single laser beam. As computers "talk" to one another over telephone circuits more and more, to relay their immense volumes of information from one part of the world to another, we'll need laser communications links merely to keep up with the tremendous demand for telephone channels. Already in the United States the telephone companies are hard pressed to provide enough circuits to keep pace with the people and computers who use the phones. Small wonder Bell Labs has been so vitally engaged in laser research!

Since laser beams are so directional, you don't waste power by spreading the beam all over the countryside when all you want to hit is a tiny receiving antenna (of course, for laser communications, antennas will be replaced by mirrors and telescopes). But, on the other hand, if you miss your receiver, the beam goes completely astray and the communications link is broken.

Very tight laser beams will also mean communications links that are quite private and difficult to eavesdrop on, since you must get directly into the beam to intercept the signal. And if an eavesdropper does stick a mirror into your beam, you'll know it instantly, because your signal will immediately either lose strength or disappear altogether.

This tight-beam privacy is a feature that the military services particularly like. They want secure communications that an enemy can't tamper with.

Weather can seriously affect a laser communications beam. Clouds, fog, rain, or snow can weaken or entirely stop a beam of visible light. In Tokyo, the Nippon Telegraph and Telephone Company has installed an experimental laser communications system. In good weather, they can easily contact receivers set up all around the vast, sprawling city. In poor weather, signals can be sent only a kilometer or two. So far, poor weather has hampered operations less than 10 percent of the time.

Carbon dioxide lasers of very high power might be able to burn right through fog and cloud, and might even be relatively unaffected by rain or snow. Of course, having laser beams of that power level squirting through the neighborhood might be slightly dangerous!

In space, there's no weather to contend with and no atmosphere to absorb the slightest amount of a laser beam's energy. The National Aeronautics and Space Administration is working hard on lasers for deep-space communications. It seems likely that when men first go to Mars, they'll send live television transmissions back to Earth on laser beams.

LASERS AS MEASURING RODS

Radar means *RA*dio *D*etection *A*nd *R*anging. If you substitute a laser for the radio equipment, you get LIDAR: *LI*ghtwave *D*etection *A*nd *R*anging. And you get many of the same advantages—and problems—of laser communications.

First, since light waves are so much smaller than radio waves, lidars can give you much more precise measurements than radars can. Where a radar signal might tell you the location of an airplane down to a few meters, lidar will tell you down to a fraction of a centimeter.

Such accuracy isn't always necessary in practical radar applications. But laser beams do make excellent "yardsticks" for measuring things very precisely. In many branches of scientific research, lasers are producing measurements of unparalleled accuracy.

As we saw in Chapter 1, lasers have bounced their

light beams off the Moon. One of the first experiments set up on the Moon by the Apollo astronauts was a laser reflector. Laser beams reflected off this equipment have allowed scientists to measure the distance to the Moon and the motions of the Moon with great precision.

Lidars are being used today as range finders. The Army is particularly fond of knowing exactly how far away a target is. And the Air Force has been using a variety of laser techniques to improve the accuracy of its bomb drops.

In a more helpful role, lidars are helping to detect and measure pollution. Laser beams can be reflected by dust and soot particles in the air that are too small to make visible smoke but are still strong enough to cause serious pollution effects. Lasers are even being used to determine the chemicals in the gases coming out of smokestacks. The laser beam is fired into the plume of gas emerging from the stack, the beam causes the various types of gas molecules to absorb the laser photons and then radiate some of this energy away. By observing the radiated energy, it is possible to tell what kinds of molecules are in the gas. Carbon monoxide, nitrous oxide, sulfur dioxide, and other pollutants can be detected in this way, even when the stack gas looks clean and the pollutants are invisible to the unaided eye.

One of the earliest practical uses of lasers has been in construction jobs and surveying, where the laser makes the best possible yardstick.

Huge tunneling machines are being guided today by tiny helium-neon lasers, which produce pencil-thin beams of light that are absolutely straight. The laser beam isn't affected by wind, uneven ground, or gravity. It stays straight. Tunnels drilled by laser-guided machines are usually straight to within a centimeter or two, while tunnels drilled with other means of guidance can drift off-center by a few centimeters every few meters. Lasers for this purpose are not only inexpensive, but they save the drilling companies a considerable amount of money by keeping the tunnel exactly on course throughout the drilling operation.

Surveyors have found lasers to be so accurate that they're beginning to do away with their traditional chains and trigonometery books. Lidar techniques are much faster and more accurate than the old method of laying out a base line and measuring angles.

Lasers are also finding interesting uses in factories, where measurements are difficult or impossible to make by other methods. For example, lasers can measure the width of red-hot strips of steel as they come out of the smelting furnaces, and make the measurement down to an accuracy of a fraction of a millimeter while the strip is moving at high speed.

Lasers also make excellent gyroscopes, which are used as part of the guidance systems in aircraft, missiles, and submarines. Honeywell, Inc., has developed tiny *ring lasers* where a beam of laser light is reflected around in an endless circle by mirrors. If the gyro is moved as little as 0.0003 degree in a second, the light beams stray off the exact center of their reflecting mirrors and cause a signal to be given off by the gyro, telling the human operators that motion has been detected. The laser gyro, which has no moving parts at all (except photons), is only a few centimeters across in size.

The same principle is used to make ultrasensitive laser seismographs, which can detect very tiny earth tremors and help geophysicists pinpoint the movements of our sometimes not-too-solid ground.

LASERS IN RESEARCH

We've already seen that lasers make excellent measuring rods, and scientists are using them as such. From measuring the distance to the Moon to measuring the speed of a hummingbird's beating wings, lasers are providing a new accuracy in many areas of research.

Holographs are allowing scientists to see things they could never see before. Laser light beams can probe into the flow of a gas, for example, without disturbing the gas flow at all. If you put an ordinary probe into the gas, even a fine wire, it would change the way in which the gas is moving. A stream of photons doesn't disturb the flow, and the photons can carry back information about the way the gas is behaving.

Do you recall that when Gabor originally hit upon the concept of holography, he wanted to improve the performance of electron microscopes? Well, laser holography is doing just that—but for optical microscopes.

One problem with microscopy is that when you go

down to very great magnifications, you lose depth of focus. You can focus on one layer of a biological cell, for example, but the rest of the cell goes out of focus. If you're looking at something that's alive, like a microscopic organism, it's difficult to get all the information you're after.

But with holography the situation changes. By taking a series of holographs with a pulsed laser, you can freeze the motion of the subject. And the holographs can be studied at leisure. Since they're three-dimensional, you can focus on any part of them you wish, and then change the focus to study another section.

Laser holography is also being used to help measure the sizes and numbers of raindrops in clouds. Scientists fly an airplane through a cloud and take holographic pictures of the raindrops. They're hoping to determine why some clouds produce rain and others don't.

LASERS AND KNOWLEDGE

Lasers have already become an indispensible tool for scientists, and they are also becoming important in many industrial uses. In their applications to computers, to communications, to measurement, lasers will bring about great changes in our lives.

There will come a day when you will have your own personal phone, small enough to fit in your pocket. You'll be able to reach almost anyone, anywhere in the world rapidly, reliably, and economically.

Your pocket phone might even have a tiny picture screen in it. At home, a book-sized computer will be keeping track of your groceries, bills, business appointments, dinner engagements, vacation plans, and much, much more.

All this tremendous flow of information will be made possible by the truly huge data capacity of lasers. Lasers will produce holographic memories in the computers and will relay the vast amounts of information that will flicker around tomorrow's world. Laser beams may be ducted through optical fiber "light pipes" here on Earth (probably underground) so that the weather won't interfere with them. And more powerful laser beams will reach out to satellites for relay across oceans and continents.

It has been said that you are what you eat. Yes, but you are also what you know. And lasers will help to make us "healthy, wealthy, and wise."

9
Microjobs and Macrojobs

When you stop to think about it, it seems almost impossible that a beam of light can cut through steel. Yet light waves *are* energy, pure and simple (well, perhaps not so simple).

We have seen that laser beams can put billions of watts of light energy on a target. And in Chapter 1 we noted that some people are already thinking about using this form of energy as a weapon.

But the laser as a source of energy will be far more useful than as a mere weapon. The laser gives us a means of putting energy into places where no other kind of tool can reach and of using that energy to do things with a precision and accuracy unachievable any other way.

MICROJOBS WITH PULSED LASERS

The first use for a laser in industry was found by Bell Telephone Laboratories. There, pulsed ruby lasers were put to work drilling holes in diamonds.

This is a serious and difficult job. Western Electric (part of the Bell system) manufactures nearly 50 million kilometers of copper wire each year, as thin as human hair. To draw such thin wire from the raw copper, the copper is heated until it is almost melted and then forced through a tiny hole in a diamond fixture called a die. Diamond is used for a simple reason: it is the hardest material known and thus resists wear the best. Even so, thousands of man-made diamonds are worn out each year at Western Electric's factories.

How do you make a tiny hole in a diamond? Diamond is not only hard, it's brittle. Western Electric formerly used miniature mechanical drills which were themselves coated with diamond dust and olive oil. Drilling a hole in a diamond die took about two days. Many of the diamonds were shattered, or the holes were too large or ragged to be useful.

Along came the pulsed ruby laser. With a few zaps of the laser, a clean, perfect-sized hole is drilled in the diamond—within minutes! The laser doesn't need any mechanical drill bits, which wear out rapidly. Of course, nothing is perfect. The laser's flash lamp burns out eventually, but it is rather easily replaced.

Soon many other jobs were found for lasers. Pulsed lasers now drill tiny holes in many different types of tough metals, for many different industries. They also are being used to smooth the surfaces of materials that are hard to polish, trim rough edges, and remove thin layers of material from tiny electronic circuit boards.

These are all jobs where only a microsocpic amount of material is to be removed. Such tasks are called *micromachining*. In this sense, the word "machining" means shaping, smoothing, or otherwise working a material such as metal or plastic.

What happens in micromachining is that the sudden pulse of laser energy that's focused down to a precise spot on the metal or plastic vaporizes some of the material it strikes. A tiny amount of the material is immediately puffed into vapor and blows away. With careful control, it is possible to remove material with a precision down to a tiny fraction of a millimeter.

Not only can the pulsed lasers remove unwanted material, they can also weld things together. Tiny electronics assemblies, where flea-sized transistors must be welded to whisker-sized wire, pose a near-impossible task for ordinary welding methods. Welding and soldering tools are just too big for the job, and they create too much heat, which might destroy the electronics parts instead of joining them together. But a pulse of laser light can put the right amount of energy exactly where you want it, with nothing hitting the target except photons. A single pulse can melt the transistor's wire connector and the tiny wire it is supposed to join with. The melt cools almost instantly, since the laser pulse lasts only a few millionths of a second, and the transistor and wire are firmly welded together.

Pulsed lasers are now also used as *microprobes* for analyzing the material that an object is made of. In this task, the problem is to find out what the object is composed of with little damage to the object itself.

For example, suppose you had the job of testing the quality of steel being produced by a mill. You could take a piece of steel as it came off the rollers and examine it by ordinary means. But this is rather slow and uses up some of the steel you want to sell.

With a pulsed laser, you could vaporize a microscopic amount of steel without stopping the production line at all and study the resulting gases by the well-known techniques of spectroscopy. Each different type of atom gives off its own "fingerprint" of spectral colors. The vaporized steel could be made to yield exact information on how much iron, chromium, carbon, tungsten, or impurities are in the sample you have tested.

Microprobes are being used in many ways and many places, including hospitals.

LASERS AS MEDICAL TOOLS

An argon laser can be used safely and effectively to remove a mole or tumor that is much darker in color than the surrounding skin area. Here monochromacity is the valuable factor. The dark area will absorb the beam, while the healthy, lighter, and more transparent tissue around it will reflect or scatter the laser light. So the unwanted tissue will be destroyed and without harming the surrounding area very much.

This same process has led to dramatic new developments of laser therapy in eye surgery. No other tool than light can enter the eye without injury. Because the lens and fluid in the eyeball are transparent, the laser light beam can go right through, without causing damage, to heat troublemaking arteries in the retina at the back of the eye. The tiny tubes are sealed quickly at that spot to block seepage that could create blindness.

Intricate and delicate microscopic finders have been devised to aim a smaller-than-pinhole beam so that it can be focused exactly on the tiny thread of artery inside the eyeball. The power of the beam and the exposure time can be precisely regulated for just the right burn. In this way, eye surgeons may save the sight of many people such as diabetics and others whose vision is threatened by disease.

More powerful lasers, such as the 10- and 100-watt argon ion lasers, are being used in experiments as "bloodless scalpels." The laser energy can not only cut through tissue like a knife, but its intense heat can seal off blood vessels by searing them as it goes by. Since the laser beam is very narrow and is moved very quickly, the patient is burned only along the thin line of the cut or incision. Laser scalpels may someday make surgery much less bloody and much better for the patient.

Pulsed lasers have been used experimentally to remove skin cancers and also spots and blemishes from the skin—including tattoos that their wearers no longer want. For these purposes, the laser is used in the same manner as the microprobes we discussed previously.

HIGH-POWER LASERS FOR BIG JOBS

The first lasers to be built, by Maiman and others, were the pulsed rubies and other pulsed crystal types. Naturally, the first industrial uses for lasers were jobs that these pulsed lasers could do, since they were the best known and most reliable.

But now that high-power CW gas lasers are becoming available and reliable, industry is starting to find important jobs for them. In a sense, the pulsed lasers found special jobs that called for microscopic precision. The high-power lasers are starting to move into big jobs, where big machinery works.

It is not hard to foresee that high-power carbon dioxide lasers will be cutting through the toughest steels at speeds that are ten or even a hundred times faster than the hottest torches can attain. All sorts of metals can and will be cut by lasers, but only when the laser becomes more efficient and therefore cheaper to use than torches or mechanical cutters.

Laser beams can also cut very brittle materials, such as certain types of plastics and glass. Mechanical cutters often shatter the piece they are trying to cut.

High-power lasers can make good welding machines too. In the aircraft industry, for example, there is a growing need to use new metals, such as titanium and beryllium, and composite materials that have boron or graphite fibers wound into their plastic structure. Such materials are difficult to weld successfully. In some cases, the metals are weakened if they mix with the oxygen in the air while being heated by the welding torch.

Laser welders can work much faster than ordinary welding machines, so that the metal is hot for very much less time. Also, the laser welding beam can be very narrow, actually heating only a tiny slice of the metal.

Powerful lasers might also be able to weaken rock to the point where it shatters. This is an important aid to drilling tunnels. At present, mechanical drills can only go a few meters a day through the hardest kinds of rock. Often the construction crews must use dynamite to break up the rock, because it is too hard for the drilling machines. This is very time-consuming and expensive. Lasers might be able to weaken the rock, or even shatter it, so that the mechanical drilling machines can simply go right along as if the rock were fairly soft.

The Department of Transportation wants to build high-speed trains that can travel almost as fast as jet planes, inside deep tunnels where they are safe from the weather. But this idea hinges on the cost of drilling deep tunnels through solid bedrock. If lasers can help make these costs reasonable, we can look forward to a system of jet trains that will link our cities swiftly and surely in all kinds of weather.

Meanwhile, back at the airport, lasers might someday be cutting holes through fog to allow planes to land safely in bad weather.

Fog is nothing more than a cloud that is close to the ground, and clouds are nothing more than collections of water droplets. High-power lasers might be able to "bake off" the water droplets, heat them to the point where they turn into water vapor, which is transparent to light. A pilot can see through water vapor (you are looking through a fair amount of water vapor right now; there is always some in the air).

LASERS AS WEAPONS

It's unpleasant to think about it, but lasers can be used as weapons. High-power carbon dioxide lasers are apparently being considered now as possible weapons by the military forces of several nations. They seem to be particularly interested in the chemical and flowing-gas electric CO_2 lasers.

The same energy that cuts through steel or helps drill tunnels might shoot down airplanes or missiles— or kill men.

As a weapon, the laser offers some great advantages. It strikes with the speed of light, of course. It is just about the only possible weapon that can strike faster than a ICBM, which travels at a top speed of nearly 20,000 kilometers per hour. Because light beams aren't bothered by gravity or wind, to aim a laser properly you merely point it at the target. There is no need to "lead" the target or worry about wind or gravity drop, which you must do with guns and even missiles.

In the December, 1970, issue of *Air Force* magazine, published by the Air Force Association (which is not part of the U.S. Government), there was an article entitled "Laser—A Weapon Whose Time Is Near." Written by Edgar E. Elsamer, associate editor of the magazine, the article said:

> Today the laser . . . is the object of a worldwide technological race . . . proceeding under extreme security precautions in the weapons area where its impact is already substantial and its future potential enormous.

The article then goes on to describe how lasers might be used to trigger hydrogen bombs, shoot down airplanes, and perform other military jobs.

If lasers can help to destroy H-bombs carrying missiles, then something truly new will have been added to the world's arsenals. Since the late 1950's, both the United States and Russia have armed themselves with fleets of ICBM's that can destroy much of the world with their bombs. Both nations have devoted huge efforts to finding a way to defend themselves against the ICBM. Lasers may help to break this deadlock of mutual terror.

In March 1983 President Ronald Regan announced that the United States was seeking ways to use high-power lasers aboard orbiting satellites as a defense against hydrogen-bomb-carrying ballistic missiles. The media soon called this idea the "Star Wars" concept. Many military experts point out that laser-carrying "battle stations" in orbit could protect the world against the threat of missile attack and nuclear war. Other experts fear that by extending military operations into space we make the Earth a more dangerous world, not less so.

This much is certain: both the U.S. and Soviet Russia are working hard on laser weaponry, and lasers fired from satellites offer a hope of stopping a nuclear missile attack. If and when such laser "battle stations" are placed in orbit, we will see dramatic changes in strategic warfare—and in the course of the world's history.

LASERS FOR FUSION

The intense beams from high-power lasers can not only trigger hydrogen bombs, they might be able to "light up" controlled fusion reactions.

In an H-bomb, the energy inside the hydrogen atom is suddenly released in a titanic explosion. The sun uses the same source of energy—hydrogen fusion—in a controlled way to produce the energy we call sunlight. Hydrogen fusion energy gives us life.

For more than thirty years, physicists have been trying to produce controlled hydrogen fusion reactions here on Earth. In this process, four hydrogen atoms are made to join together—to fuse—into a single helium atom. In doing this, the atoms release energy.

If controlled fusion reactors could be built, they would use for fuel the atoms of a special form of hydrogen, called *deuterium*. There's enough deuterium in the oceans to provide more than a million times more electrical power than the whole world uses today—and provide it for millions upon millions of years!

In other words, fusion reactors could produce all the power man needs for his homes, his factories, his cities, his farms—power to desalt ocean water and irrigate the deserts—cheap, reliable power, without pollution. Nuclear fusion power can help to eliminate poverty and hunger, maybe eliminate the causes of war.

If high-power lasers can help to make successful fusion reactors possible, it will be the most important contribution to man's well-being that any invention can make. Such a happy future would far outweigh the laser's possible uses as a weapon.

10
The Bright Promise

We end almost exactly where we started, with the vision of H. G. Wells's evil Martians and their death-dealing heat ray. But we know now that such a beam of energy can do far more good than harm if men use it wisely.

When lasers were first invented in 1960, there was tremendous enthusiasm among scientists and engineers throughout the world. The new invention was so different, so exciting, it was hailed as the answer to almost every problem that could be thought of.

Then it turned out that the earliest lasers couldn't solve everybody's problems. In fact, within a few

221

years after it first appeared, the laser was being described as "a solution in search of a problem." Slowly, scientists and engineers began to find problems that lasers could solve. And as we've seen, they developed new lasers, more powerful, more reliable, that could face up to even tougher problems.

There is one use for a pulsed laser that is very dear to the heart of a writer: the laser eraser. Schawlow figured out this idea.

When you make a mistake in typing, a carefully aimed pulse of laser energy can make a beautiful, quick, and easy erasure. The black ink of the letter you want removed will absorb the laser energy. The white paper will tend to reflect any laser light that strikes it. When the ink absorbs the energy, its temperature instantly rises and it vaporizes, blows away. The paper isn't bothered at all. Neither are the letters on either side of the one you've removed. Compared to the messy job of rubbing out a mistake or painting it over with white ink, the laser eraser is a writer's dream.

Unfortunately, no one has produced a laser eraser that's cheap enough to sell in stationery stores—or anywhere else. As far as I know, Schawlow himself has the only one in existence, and he built it himself.

However, lasers *are* being built and sold and put to work in factories, hospitals, schools, and research laboratories. Lasers may someday help to defend us against missile attack and might even make the golden dream of controlled hydrogen fusion power a reality. Lasers may help to cure certain types of cancer, and they'll probably go with the men who fly to Mars.

This field of laser research and development is moving so rapidly that parts of this book will be out of date even as you read.

All of this has happened because an army of men, over the past three centuries or so, have asked themselves, "What is light?" We still don't have a complete answer. But we have all had a lot of excitement trying to find it.